# An Unfinished Story

Erica Haraldsen

# An Unfinished Story

By Erica Haraldsen

This novel is a work of fiction from the author's imagination. Characters, stories, and names are fiction. Location names are real and are only used to provide a sense of authenticity but the described environment of the location is a work of fiction.

An Unfinished Story. Copyright © 2020 Erica Haraldsen.
Originally created by Erica Haraldsen, 2019.
All rights reserved. No part of this book may be used or reproduced without consent from the author.
For information about permission to reproduce sections of this book, email ericaharaldsen@gmail.com
First Edition.

ISBN 979-8-63-601565-9

Erica Haraldsen

You never know how gentle encouragement can change your life. Thank you L.N. for nudging me toward writing my book.

Thank you K.H. and C.M. for cheering me on the entire way. The constructive feedback has been monumental.

Thank you C.G. for formatting my book. Without you, it would still be sitting in my chromebook.

# Chapter 1

It was a hot and humid day in Boston. The city was bustling with people intermingling in all directions. People were scurrying to the nearest train station, hurrying to get to work on time and leisurely walking to class. Boston was full of young people, Joanie noticed. Young people who have their entire lives in front of them. A life of making mistakes, learning, growing, and hopefully not falling into the same rut she did. When she went to college, she thought a business degree was the answer to money and money would lead her to happiness. Now, she was sitting in a cubicle eight hours a day managing a team of young reporters for the local newspaper. She knew the minutes were ticking down before newspapers became obsolete. People preferred to get their news from social media and the internet rather than hold an actual paper to see what was going on in the world.

She had been unhappy at work for years but the benefits were great, and honestly, what else would she do? She had been pigeonholed into print media for so long, she didn't feel valuable in any other area of commerce. Sure, there were many options within Boston, but who would hire her? She had no fashion sense, didn't wear makeup, and was past her prime for television media. It was just easier to stay put and live a mundane life of cubicles, the sound of typing, and deadlines. Life was easier when you remained loyal and committed to your decisions. At least it was a steady paycheck for now.

Joanie prided herself in her ability to live alone in the very expensive metropolitan area. It was almost a badge of honor

## An Unfinished Story

to prove to those around her that she was successful enough to live the posh life in Boston. No one had to know that her cabinets were filled with boxes of Macaroni and Cheese and cereal and her freezer was filled with frozen pizza and ice cream. There was no one there to judge her, so she often sat alone eating dinner in front of the television.

Joanie was never one for people. She found small talk irritating and fatiguing. It was hard for her to know what questions were expected to be asked, how much information to give about herself, and how to gently exit a conversation without being rude. Living alone and not venturing into the city on weekends was much less stressful. Her life felt predictable, safe, and ordinary and Joanie thought that predictable, safe and ordinary would make her feel content. Somehow, as she approached her 40th birthday, she felt sad, disappointed, and unfulfilled by how things unfolded so far.

As Joanie walked into the building, a wave of cool air greeted her and Joanie stood in front of the central air vent with gratitude. She gave a quick wave to the building attendant and made her way to the elevator. Joanie had a meeting scheduled with her boss, Mark, which wasn't unusual for a Monday morning. Every Monday they sat down together and talked about the weekend events and what topics to target. Joanie was in charge of the Lifestyle section, which usually meant eight to twelve stories were run on Sundays. It was a fun section to assign because oftentimes it required her staff to go out and talk to people about what they thought was important. It required research and personal interaction, which helped keep her department upbeat and cheerful. Plus, the topics weren't exactly life shattering, so writing about the rise of coffee shops and the fall of bookstores wasn't quite as stressful as writing about the latest tornado to hit the midwest. Joanie's job was to assign the topics to the staff, read and edit their writing, and make sure everything was in by the deadline.

Joanie entered Mark's office and found the entire department crammed around the conference table. Some people were standing, some were sitting, and some were wedged in between the filing cabinets. Joanie felt surprised and concerned. Usually these meetings were for the department heads only. "What is going on?" Joanie asked no one in particular.

The young, blond intern, whose name Joanie couldn't remember, whispered, "Rumor has it, the newspaper might be bought out." The blonde intern continued to jabber away, but Joanie couldn't quite follow what she was saying. That couldn't be right. Joanie just got a raise. Surely they wouldn't do that if the newspaper wasn't doing well, would they?

As the young, bubbly intern spoke about the rumors she heard, how she was going to change her major first thing tomorrow, and how she wasn't going to tell her parents about the internship because no one believed she would make it in the media anyway, the group around her started mumbling all at once. The room suddenly went from quiet to cacophonous. Even though Joanie couldn't read their lips or hear their words, she could read their faces, and there was concern among them all.

As a department head, she felt she needed to do something to stop the chaos. Joanie looked around the room and tried to wave her arms and raise her voice above the mumbling and grumbling. Nothing worked. She was pressed into the water cooler and her petite frame was blocked by the filing cabinet adjacent to her.

The lights flickered three times. Suddenly it was quiet. There was no movement. Everyone turned to the door, and there stood Mark in his short but stocky stature. He couldn't quite make it into the room or squeeze himself in between the conference chairs and wall, so he pulled a chair in from the lobby and stood on the seat. "Attention everyone!" he bellowed. "I have some news to share". He wasn't smiling but his voice carried confidence, as if he had been practicing this speech all morning. His brow line was furrowed and he had purple bags under his eyes. His clothes were disheveled, and Joanie noticed he was wearing one black and one navy blue shoe. His physical presentation did not match the way

## An Unfinished Story

he delivered his message. Joanie made eye contact and smiled, trying to emit reassurance to whatever message he was sending.

"As you know, the newpaper numbers have been steadily decreasing over the past eight years," Mark started. "Our business manager met with me last week and reviewed the financial numbers with me. Unfortunately, it doesn't look good and we will be filing bankruptcy. Not just us, but the entire company. People are no longer getting their news through print. Everything is online and even with online viewing, people aren't paying for the online exclusive membership. We just don't have the numbers to support continued print media, or any sort of media for that matter. I suppose if we get bought out, we may have the ability to keep some of our jobs through a transfer to the new company. But if bankruptcy goes through, we all will be searching the help wanted ads. I am sorry. I will be meeting with all of you individually to discuss your options but I wanted you all to hear the news at once. Please go back to work and continue your day as planned. You are all dismissed."

As quickly as he appeared, he was gone. The chair was gone and the silence was gone. Just as before, noise erupted within the tiny conference room. Joanie was surprised but not shocked. She knew this day would come, she just didn't believe it would happen today. She exited the room and slowly walked back to her desk, hiding behind her cubicle. She placed her head in her hands and thought about all the time and years spent within the confines of these four walls.

She thought about the day she got the job. She started off as a young, enthusiastic, aspiring twenty-one year old, excited to start her first internship in college. All she did for those six months was get coffee, order lunch for her supervisor Mikayla, shred paper and file articles, but she didn't care. She had her foot in the door and this was going to be the start of something. She worked hard during college and gave her all to every internship her program threw at her. As she walked the stage at graduation, she knew she was destined for great things.  She was filled with confidence and pride and was ready to take on the world.

After Joanie graduated from college, she applied to every newspaper, magazine, and online journalism outlet she could find within a thirty mile radius.  After six months of rejection after rejection after rejection, Joanie accepted a job waitressing and bartending to pay the bills.  After one excruciating night, she stepped off the subway train and found three young men who grabbed her purse and ran.  The very next day Joanie quit her job.  She was broke and scared and needed to do something.  She reached out to Mikayla and asked if there was anything open at the paper.

Mikayla didn't respond to Joanie's email for five days and those five days were tough.  First Joanie thought Mikayla was busy and just hadn't gotten around to it, then Joanie thought Mikayla was ignoring her for not keeping in touch more consistently, and then Joanie thought Mikayla had no idea who she was and had deleted her email.  Joanie fretted around her house for days afraid to go out after dark, applied to retail jobs, applied to administrative assistant jobs, and hid all the incoming mail.  On day five, Joanie heard the familiar ding of her email and sucked in her breath when she saw Mikayla's name in the sender line.  She was scared to open it. What if Mikayla had no idea who she was?  What if Mikayla had interns after her that were more organized, more chipper, and more hard working than Joanie?  What if Mikayla felt bad for her for not getting a job sooner?  Joanie closed her eyes and clicked the email open.

*Hi Joanie!* Joanie read in Mikayla's voice.  *It was so great to hear from you.  Sorry it took so long for me to get back to you, I was asking around to see if anyone needed additional help in their departments.  There is an opening for a part time Lifestyle reporter, if you were interested in applying.  It's not a lot of hours, but it is a paid position.  You can find the job description below and the link to apply.  Please let me know if you have any questions.  Mikayla Moore, Editor.*  Joanie slammed down her laptop screen and started jumping up and

## An Unfinished Story

down with excitement. She had a wide grin plastered across her face and had to forcefully relax her lips because her cheeks were starting to burn. Yes, yes yes! Joanie thought. Finally, an opportunity to get her career on the right path! Part time? Who cares! A job is a job is a job! Joanie grabbed a fresh cup of coffee, opened her laptop and started the application process.

And that defining moment, when life seemed full of opportunity, possibility, and growth, was fifteen long years ago.

# Chapter 2

"Would you like tea or coffee today?" Carly asked the young couple sitting in her dining room. They were on their honeymoon, enjoying the rocky coastline of Block Island. The waves were crashing against the coast, as high tide was slowly creeping in. The sun had already been up for a few hours, as had Carly. Every morning she rose at 4:30 with the sunrise to prepare breakfast for the morning guests.

This was actually a slower week, and Carly thought it maybe had to do with the drop in number of ferry rides connecting the island to the mainland. Carly had three rooms to clean and care for this weekend, and none of the guests had small children, which was nice and relaxing but also too quiet. Carly enjoyed sharing all her favorite kid spots with the families who chose to stay with her. Carly grew up on the island, so it was fun to share her favorite places and the special hideaways that tourists rarely stumbled upon.

Carly worked the room with a coffee pot in one hand and a teapot in the other. She loved to ask the guests about their lives back home. What did they do for work? Where did they live? Why did they come to Block Island? Block Island was a tiny island off the coast of Rhode Island near the tip of Long Island. Martha's Vineyard and Nantucket were more famous than Block Island so Carly always found it interesting to see why people chose to come here instead of the others.

"Emma, how has your weekend been so far?" Carly asked the young newlywed sitting at the small table facing the large picture window. Emma smiled up at Carly while cupping the hot teacup in her hand and commented on the beautiful

## An Unfinished Story

scenery, kind people, and delicious seafood. Carly smiled back because when people had a great time on vacation, they usually gave positive reviews online. Positive reviews meant more business, which meant more money in her pocket.

She worked her way around the room and chatted noncommittally with a retired couple from New Jersey and a single woman who was a photographer on the side. Seeing as how it was Sunday, all three rooms were checking out that day. Carly knew she had a busy day cleaning, restocking the fridge, doing laundry, and tending to the garden. Sundays were her favorite day of the week because it allowed her to reflect on her guests' experiences, decompress from the weekend, and brainstorm on ways to make the next round of guests' experiences even better.

When the last guest checked out for the day, Carly flopped on the sofa within her private living space. The temperature was predicted to hit 90 today with a wet, humid feel. Sometimes, when all the guests had left and she was faced with the task of cleaning, an overwhelming sense of dread enveloped her and killed her motivation. Instead of jumping to the dishes, Carly turned on the television, grabbed a cup of tea, and fell into the world of reality television.

Sometimes she wondered what life would have been like if she left the island right out of high school and never returned. All her friends left, but her quickly aging parents put a wrinkle in her plans. When Carly's parents were in their 40's, the double line on the pregnancy stick was the surprise of their life. They felt too old to bring a child into the world. They had a successful business and a predictable routine and children were never part of the plan. How would they manage juggling the life of a child and running a business at their age? Of course they were surprised, overwhelmed, and scared, but decided that they would do the best they could to give their baby the life it deserved. Carly was that baby and no other babies followed.

The problem came when Carly hit her 30th birthday. Her parents were older than some of her friends' grandparents.

## Erica Haraldsen

Her parents lived a life of busyness and fatigue running this bed and breakfast, which eventually impacted their health. The day before Carly's 30th birthday, her dad, Peter, had a heart attack. He was in the yard mowing the grass. Her mother was at the market restocking on fresh fruit and vegetables. The doctor said it was instant but Carly often wondered if that was true. Maybe if they lived on the mainland, the proximity to a hospital and good doctors would have saved him.

Carly had moved to Maine when she was in her late twenties to the chagrin of her parents. They needed her help managing the bed and breakfast but knew that they had to let her go explore life on her own terms. They tried not to depend on her too much or burden her with the daily stressors on the island. When Carly's father passed away, she had been living in Maine with a lobster fisherman and she knew that her mom couldn't run the business on her own. Her mom barely had time to grieve, what with the busy summer months full of bookings ahead of her. So Carly returned home. Just for the summer. Just to get her mom back into the routine. Just to help. But she never left.

When Carly was 36, her mom, Ruth, turned 78. Her mother wasn't feeling well and had an appointment with the local doctor but never made it to him. She ended up having a stroke, which made her have trouble walking, talking, and feeding herself. Ruth had been diagnosed with mild dementia five years prior, so between the two ailments, she could no longer care for herself. Carly couldn't take care of her either. Her mom went to the nursing home just a ferry ride away and had been there ever since. That was three and a half years ago. Carly struggled with whether or not she could go back to Maine and back to the life she adored. She decided to stay on the island and take over the legacy her parents left her, just until Ruth passed away. After that, Carly planned on returning to her old life and hoped that it would be an easy transition. Carly visited Ruth every Wednesday. She transported Ruth's

## An Unfinished Story

laundry back and forth, brought her gifts and snacks, and tried her best to make the end of her life as best as it could be.

Carly had a choice when her mom got sick. She could try and convince Ruth to sell the Willowside B & B and move back to Maine or hang on to it and try to make it work. Her mother would have been devastated if she sold it, so Carly decided the best thing to do was hang onto it until her mother died and then sell. Once Ruth was gone, there was no reason to feel guilty for throwing her family's livelihood away. Carly wasn't wishing for that day, but she knew that she was approaching forty and probably missed her opportunity to follow her dreams. When this place sold, Carly would be ecstatic that she wasn't trapped in her old life but sad to turn the page on this very long chapter in her life.

# Chapter 3

Joanie sat in front of her computer staring at the Google home screen. She was paralyzed, unsure of what to search for. Should she look for a new job? New apartment? New roommate? She knew, as of today, she still had a job, but the uncertainty of it, with no savings in place, was giving her a headache. Her family was under the impression that she was living an amazing life in an amazing city, with an amazing career in place. If she told them that her house of cards was going to crumble at any given moment, shame and embarrassment would wash over her. She would feel like such a failure.

Joanie closed her computer and decided it could wait another day. In the meantime, she would look for a second job to put some money away. Should she find a roommate? That would be a terrible idea, Joanie decided, unless it was absolutely necessary. Joanie would rather live in her sister's basement than live with a stranger.

It was Saturday, the day after the big announcement and the sun was shining. The weatherman forecasted hot weather with less humidity. Joanie wiped her brow just anticipating the heat that was going to develop over the next few days.

Mark had given her a summer assignment for the LIfestyle section of the paper. Joanie usually delegated assignments to her teammates and didn't understand why Mark was offering her this task. He explained that she was one of the most senior employees and deserved some fun. Plus, she didn't have a husband or kids so there wouldn't be any

## An Unfinished Story

logistical factors that interfered with the assignment being completed.

For the next eight weeks, Joanie was going to document the pros and cons of island living, as judged by the community. Joanie had three choices: Martha's Vineyard, Nantucket, or Block Island. All three locations entailed almost a full day of travel. With Joanie being in charge of the Lifestyle section, she knew she needed to either only travel on the weekends or work remotely from the island (whichever island she decided). Working remotely would be fine as long as wi-fi was adequate. But then her apartment would be empty, which really made her nervous.

Joanie had never been to any of those three islands. She knew that Martha's Vineyard and Nantucket were extremely pricey and the cost to stay overnight would be high. The newspaper was struggling so Joanie felt a responsibility to be money-conscious when searching for accommodations. She knew very little about Block Island, but her sister's boyfriend was from there, so maybe he knew of something or someone who could house her for a few weeks. She made a mental note to give her sister a call.

In the meantime, Joanie reopened her laptop and searched for Block Island, Nantucket, and Martha's Vineyard. She looked at cost: the ferry ride, accommodations, things to do, and food. This assignment was a Hail Mary to get more people interested in the paper, but Joanie felt that it was a death sentence. Was Mark trying to exhaust all funds before the sale? Was he trying to make the paper go bankrupt? Joanie decided that it didn't really matter and that she was just following orders. If he wanted to waste the last of the money the paper had on a "vacation", then who was she to question it? She would take her assignment seriously, do her best to make the paper proud, and live like a local.

Joanie opened her laptop and continued researching. Seeing as how she was going to be staying overnight, the cost of accommodations was crucial. She found that all three islands presented the same issues. Bustling environment in the summer and isolated environment in the off season. It seemed that fishing, tourism, and old family wealth were the main reasons people stayed year round.

Joanie decided that the cost of accommodation would be the final factor in where she was going to crash for the next few months. But seeing how summer already started, it appeared that she wasn't going to be able to be selective in her final arrangement. Joanie joined random PeoplePlace groups for all three locations to ask questions and get leads about where to stay. She continued to do research, went to the library, and drove to the coast of Rhode Island and the shore of Cape Cod to chat it up with locals who had a different view of life on the islands. Her gut instinct was telling her that Block Island was the direction to focus her attention on, so Joanie did just that.

*******************************************************************************************************

"Welcome to The Willowside!" Carly exclaimed, reaching for the designer luggage the young man was holding. He and a woman, his wife Carly presumed, entered the home with a big smile on their face.

"Hello!" the young woman exclaimed. "We are so happy to be here! Where is your bathroom?" Carly quickly checked their reservation and showed them to their room, which had an ensuite bathroom. This couple, Jason and Rachael Jones, were staying for the weekend. They were from Long Island, New York, and traveled a far distance by car and ferry. It was only 10 am, but they were probably ready to take a nap from waking up in the early morning. They were celebrating their three year anniversary. Carly loved hearing about the lives of her visitors. Every story seemed so magical and more exciting than her own.

Carly had a total of four guests she needed to check in today. Waiting for everyone to check in was the hardest part of her day because of the uncertainty of when they would arrive. Carly would love to be able to go for a run, or go to the

## An Unfinished Story

grocery store, or sit outside in her garden and get dirty with the Earth, but she had to make sure she was presentable and mentally prepared to greet and welcome all her guests. Repeat customers and word of mouth were what made her business successful and she needed to make sure that every experience was a positive one. That meant that no one had to wait when they arrived. Carly busied herself in the kitchen making fresh blueberry muffins and coffee while she waited for the others to arrive. Carly knew that when Mr. and Mrs. Jones returned from getting settled upstairs, the coffee and muffins would be done.

Carly sat at the table while waiting for the timer on the microwave to ding, indicating that her delicious muffins were done cooking. Carly thought of all the things she needed to do that week. Pay the bills. Go grocery shopping. Laundry. Yardwork. Visit her mother. Read Tripadvisor reviews and comments. Her list didn't seem long, but it was still causing her anxiety. Her anxiety always seemed to grow when she wasn't able to accomplish anything due to waiting around for guests. Carly took a deep breath and listened to the sound of the waves and the birds chirping, creating a melody of their own.

When Carly was a little girl she dreamed of living away from the island. The constant lap of water against the shore was always soothing to Carly, so she knew that no matter where she lived, she would need to be near the ocean. It helped clear the cobwebs of her mind when life seemed overwhelming. Carly moved to Maine because she needed a change. She knew that Portland was small enough of a city that she wouldn't feel lost but big enough of a city that she could make herself lost if needed. Every morning, she would walk along the shoreline and watch the sun rise. She would think about her parents but knew that Block Island was no place to settle down.

Carly met John, a lobster fisherman, when she was twenty-eight. She was waitressing at a quaint seafood restaurant in the middle of the city and he would often deliver fresh lobsters on Thursday, Saturday, and Tuesday. Carly was working almost every day during the summer season and would sign off on John's deliveries.

John was attractive, Carly decided, in a rugged and rough way. He had long dark hair, a goatee, and often wore cargo shorts and a t-shirt. He appeared to be a simple man. Carly wasn't interested at first, but as she got to know him, he felt more and more attractive to her. She slipped him her phone number on a sticky note in the middle of July, and from that point forward, they were an item.

It happened fast, but they were living together by December and stayed together until Carly's dad died. She knew she would have to make a difficult decision because Portland, Maine and Block Island were not exactly commutable. It would be a whole day of traveling between the ferry, the drive, and getting through Boston traffic, so they decided to take a break. Being a lobsterman was all John knew, and yes, Block Island is surrounded by ocean, but lobster isn't nearly as prevalent as it is in Maine. That was nine years ago. They kept in touch for a while, but life moved fast and eventually they both moved on. Carly thought about Maine often and wondered if John was still in the same apartment doing the same job with the same people. Probably not, she thought. Carly hoped that he had found a woman he loved and settled down. She hoped he was happy.

Carly's phone rang. "Willowside B and B," Carly spoke into the phone.

"Hi, can I please speak to the owners?" a deep voice on the other end of the line asked.

"This is Carly. How can I help you today?" Carly replied.

"Carly! Hey! This is Chris Carter, your old neighbor." Carly immediately recognized his voice and imagined the eight year old boy riding his bike up and down the hills into town to get ice cream with her. They spent many days riding their bikes all over the island solving mysteries that they created in their imagination. Carly remembered the one time they were peeking into old Mrs. Crandell's living room window to find her

## An Unfinished Story

staring back at them with her thin frame, dark beady eyes, and wild white hair. The two of them screamed in shock, jumped on their bikes, and rode home so fast that they collapsed in the driveway. Carly's parents made them write an apology note to Mrs. Crandell promising that they would never look in her windows again. Carly chuckled to herself at the memory. Chris moved off the island after high school to go to college and never returned. His parents sold their home for millions once all the kids moved out and they retired down south. Carly never saw him again.

"Wow! Chris! It's been years! How have you been?" she quickly responded.

Carly and Chris spoke for a while catching up on island life. Who was still living? Who passed away? Why was she back? Carly didn't want to go into the entire story, so she told him that it was best for her family and best for the business. After a few minutes of chatting, Chris revealed the purpose of his phone call.

"Carly, I have a favor to ask you. A favor from one friend to another." Carly waited on the other end, not quite sure where this conversation was going. It had been almost twenty years since they last spoke or saw each other. What type of favor could she possibly do for him? "I know a girl" Chris continued, "who needs a place to stay for a while and she can't afford summer rates. It's actually my girlfriend's sister."

"Why does she need a place to stay?" Carly interrupted him. "Is she in trouble with money or the law?" She laughed at the joke but her thoughts immediately went to all the crime and law television shows she watched over the years. She imagined drugs, prostitution, teen pregnancy, abusive husband...there were so many potential reasons why someone needed a place to stay on a remote island.

"Oh, it's nothing like that!" Chris laughed. "She works for a paper and they gave her a summer assignment to investigate island life around New England. She knew I was from Rhode Island, so she thought I might know someone who could help her out."

## Erica Haraldsen

A summer assignment, Carly thought. What exactly does that mean? She talked to Chris about the details. Her rooms were going for three hundred dollars a night on the weekends and two hundred seventy five dollars a night during the work week. That was a lot of money to potentially throw away during the busiest time of the year. Chris convinced Carly that she wasn't going on vacation, she was going to immerse herself in life. Chris pointed out that it could be an amazing opportunity for her business to spread and grow. This reporter would be reporting on her experiences, and eventually, somewhere in her writing, she would name the place where she was staying and most likely review it.

Carly had to really think about it. If she let a stranger stay in one of her rooms for the entire summer, she would lose too much money. She didn't even know if there would be room since reservations were booked so far in advance. Carly couldn't have her staying in the main house. It was too risky and if Carly was ever going to get off this island, she needed all the money she could get. There was a carriage house set behind the main house that had been empty for years. Carly knew that if she ever got around to fixing it up, it would be an amazing private addition to her business but life seemed to get in the way and the carriage house continued to sit. The house wasn't in great shape, but it did have walls, wooden floors, and an old bathroom straight out of the 1970s. Definitely not up to tourism standards, but beggars can't be choosers, and this could be livable with a little love. This would be perfect for our reporter, Carly thought, in case she turned out to have a second identity or be a serial killer.

Carly told Chris that yes, she could stay, but the accommodations weren't great, and that she would need to help out around the bed and breakfast if she wanted to stay for free. Carly thought about the hours it took to wash all the linens when she could be doing something else. She thought about grocery shopping in the tiny market with hundreds of tourists who were paralyzed by sticker shock. She thought about all the time spent waiting around for guests to arrive or

## An Unfinished Story

check out when her to-do list was growing by the second. Yes, Carly told Chris, this could be good. She had one week to clear all the debris and junk from the carriage house when her new roommate would arrive.

**********************************************************************************************************

"You what?" Joanie looked at Chris's big smile and gave him a hug. She looked at her sister, Maria, and said, "I cannot believe he did that." Chris contacted a girl whom he hadn't spoken to in twenty years for her. Joanie knew, firsthand, how difficult that must have been because how do you naturally start conversation? Hello ...I know it's been half our life, but can you spare a room for free for the summer? She could only imagine how awkward their conversation must have been.

Chris told her she had a week to pack a bag and get down there. He told her she was in the carriage house, which sounded very Victorian and romantic. Joanie could only imagine the big windows, stained glass, and birds chirping outside the windows. Chris told her that his friend, when he knew her in high school, was always busy. She was on the Yearbook committee, played sports, played an instrument, and was the first class president the school ever had for their measly graduating class of nine students. To Joanie, she sounded like a nightmare. Well, at least she will have a whole building to herself, she thought, and contact should be minimal.

Joanie asked Chris if she would have to pay for the room, and he told her it was free for the summer. He mentioned that she would have to help out here and there, but Joanie thought that would be great material for her articles. Joanie was planning on staying four consecutive days a week so she could check in on her plants, pop into the office, drop off her articles, make sure her team was actually working, and make sure her apartment was still standing. Even if this was the worst experience of her life, she thought, it would be over in 8 short weeks. All she had to do was get through July and August.

She met with Mark that afternoon and told him the assignment was a go. She told him she knew a guy who knew a girl so the newspaper wouldn't have to pay any money for her housing. She googled The Willowside B&B and felt comfortable with what she saw. A big colonial home with white siding, black shutters, and a red door. There were trees in the front yard providing ample shade for a swinging bench that sat next to the house. There was a big black and white sign with the name in delicate cursive. The breakfast room had two tables set up with plain decor and the rooms had queen and king size beds with fluffy pillows and bedsheets. It looked fancier than Joanie felt comfortable with, but she reminded herself that she wasn't staying in this house. She searched for the owner, and found a quick biography on Carly Davis. Carly Davis looked to be in her mid-thirties with straight blonde hair, straight, white teeth, and bright blue eyes. She looked like a cheerleader, Joanie decided. Joanie clicked on the email link, because if they were going to be living together for the next 8 weeks, it was time that they were introduced.

*Hi Carly,* Joanie typed. *My name is Joanie Wilson, and Chris is my sister's boyfriend. I wanted to thank you for letting me stay with you this summer. I was wondering, is there anything I need to bring? Sheets, towels, blankets, food? I know you are doing me a favor, so I am willing to do whatever you need me to do to help you. Thank you so much for everything. I can't wait to meet you! --Joanie.* Joanie hit send and looked around her quiet, minimal apartment.

She watered her plants and plucked off the dead leaves. Studies showed that speaking to your plants would help them live and Joanie thought for sure that if her plants were ever going to be mad at her, it would be now. She thought of all the things she had to do before Friday. She needed to go to the post office and put in a vacation hold, empty her trash, and leave on a light so no one would know she wasn't home. This is ridiculous, she thought. I am going away for four day

## An Unfinished Story

stretches, not four months. Joanie scratched the post office idea. It's totally appropriate to have mail sit in the mailbox all week. Plus, it was a locked mailbox. If it got too full, the postman would leave her a note to come pick it up. Joanie took a deep breath, told herself it would be fine, and went into the office to tell Mark that she planned to tell her staff about her summer plans and how she would manage them from afar.

Mark stood in his office with his hands against his waist, smiling down at her. He couldn't believe that she found a place to live for free. This was better than he ever could have expected. When he originally assigned this assignment to Joanie, he thought it would be a good way to keep her engaged in the paper and possibly attract new readers. After she agreed, he thought about how different summer and winter life can be for the islands. He decided that if the paper was still around and this summer series was a success in terms of readership and followers, he would send her back in the winter just to give his readers another perspective.

"Wonderful!" Mark clapped his hands. "Be sure to save all your receipts including the ferry rides, food shopping, drinks when you go out to chat with the locals, and any island activities you do. Save everything. The paper will reimburse you on the 1st and the 15th of the month once you go over the cash advance." Joanie looked at him blankly. She didn't think about how she was actually going to survive out there in the middle of summer during the busiest, most expensive time. She didn't have any money. She looked at the calendar and realized that July 1st was ten days away. She could probably survive the next ten days without using any of her own money. "Okay. Thanks" she distractedly replied. She walked out of his office holding reimbursement forms and headed toward her cubicle.

On her desk was a small bouquet of flowers with a card that said, "It's 5:00 somewhere" and was signed by her team. Joanie smiled to herself. She wished she was going to a tropical island somewhere where the water was clear, snorkeling was a thing to do, and the weather never dropped below 80. That type of place was not where she was going, but at least it was better than the summer in Boston.

    Joanie rounded up the team members who were there and made her announcement. "Obviously, you already know I took on a summer assignment on Block Island, but that does not mean I will not be around. I am always available via telephone or email. I will be checking into the office once a week to meet with you and to make sure you are prepared for the paper. While I am gone, please go to Mikayla or Mark with any questions. They will be overseeing the print organization and will be assigning you your topics. You will send me your finished articles and I will send everything to Mikayla to prepare the articles for printing. I might be in the office less, but I am still here, still part of the team, and still available if you need anything. Remember, I am just a ferry ride away." A ferry ride and a three hour car ride, Joanie thought to herself, but who's counting? She thanked them for the flowers, packed up her contact list for the team and for the managers, her notebook, her lucky pen, and went home to pack.

# Chapter 4

What was I thinking? Carly thought to herself. Why would I allow a complete stranger to stay at my house in the middle of the summer for free? If my parents were still around, they would kill me. Carly looked at the carriage house and sighed. She was overwhelmed by the mess and didn't even know where to begin. There was a bed, a dresser, a small kitchenette area, a couch, and a bathroom. It definitely wasn't the nicest place, but with a little love, it could be beautiful. Time of course was not plentiful so the level of love she could give this place was minimal. This reporter, whom Carly couldn't remember her name, was arriving Monday. Thankfully Carly didn't have anyone else checking in until Friday.

    The last time anyone stayed at this guest house was twenty years ago. Carly came home from Maine with her boyfriend in tow, and because they were not married, her parents did not want them staying in the same bedroom. Sure, they weren't married, but they were living together, so in their relationship married was just a word. Her parents refused to let them take up any bedrooms in the bed and breakfast, so they were forced to use a bedroom in the carriage house or they would have to find another room somewhere else. Carly and John were broke. They could barely afford the ferry ride over or the gas to get home, so John slept in the carriage house and Carly slept on the couch in her parent's living quarters.

    It wasn't the visit she was expecting. Her father was interested in John's work but told Carly he seemed a little

## An Unfinished Story

rough around the edges. Carly thought it was the dirty jeans, long beard and mustache that threw her dad off. John sat on a fishing boat for months on end in the cold, windy water. He smelled like fish every time he came home. From Carly's perspective, he was wearing clean jeans compared to what she usually had to wash. John felt more comfortable in clothes that were broken in and comfortable. As for the beard, Carly thought, it was meant to keep him warm.

Her mother didn't trust him. Carly's grandfather had been a fisherman off the coast of Block Island, and because of the lifestyle, the lack of sleep for months on end, and the stress of not knowing if there would be enough money to pay the rent or buy food, Carly's grandfather resorted to drinking his worries away. Since he drank in his free time, they didn't have enough money for food and often resorted to traditional Irish boiled dinners because it was all they could afford. By not having a variety of meat, it reinforced his fear of not being able to provide for his family, which led to increased drinking to deal with his fears. In private, Carly's mother often asked about John's drinking habits. Carly knew where the questions were stemming from, but it still bothered her that her mother didn't trust her decision making skills, especially when it came to a partner.

John stayed in the carriage house during their last trip home. It was a weekend full of tension, side eye glances, and double intention sighs. Carly got tired of defending her boyfriend so they left a day early. This carriage house brought back many memories and emotions of that trip and Carly decided to let it go. She was going to do her best to clean it up, make it acceptable, and welcome her guest with a clean, clutter free space that didn't hold any memories.

Carly grabbed the linens on the bed and threw them into the donate pile. No one needed floral patterns from 1992. She grabbed the towels in the kitchenette and linen closet and smelled them. Mildew and dust. Lovely. Into the donate pile they went. She looked at the curtains more closely. They were definitely faded from the sun and covered in dust. She looked in the bathroom.  The shower curtain was pea green and had mildew climbing up the bottom.  Gone gone gone.  Carly needed to turn this guest house into a place that contained zero memories of her childhood or her parents.

Carly rewashed all the dishes and made a list of what she needed to buy at SuperMart.  Toilet paper, paper towels, curtains, sheets, pillows, a new blanket, bathroom accessories, a new trash can, and a few decor pictures made the list.  She pulled everything off the walls and put them in the basement, vacuumed the rugs, dusted the surfaces, and febreezed every place you could sit or sleep.  After a long day, Carly sat down and looked around.  The place could definitely use a little paint but there was no time for that.  She looked at the pile of items to be donated and carried them down into the basement.  There really was no place to donate on the island and there was no way she was going to transfer all the stuff to the mainland today.  She brought all the trash to the dumpster and decided she did enough work for one day.  Tomorrow she would spend time on the mainland at SuperMart finishing the carriage house for her guest.

*********************************************************************
*********************************

Joanie didn't know what to do.  Do islanders own a car?  Having a car transported to and from Block Island was rather expensive.  If she didn't bring her car over, how in the world would she get home?  Joanie did some research and found that to bring a car back and forth would cost 80 dollars per round trip.  That would be about 650 dollars for the summer.  Or she could park her car at port on the mainland for 15 dollars per day, which would cost 60 dollars per week or 480 dollars for the summer.  Of course the paper was paying, but initially, Joanie was covering the cost.  She would have to drop off her receipts for reimbursement immediately because she definitely didn't have an extra 100 dollars in her account every week.

# An Unfinished Story

Joanie felt her heart rate increase and her palms sweat as she thought about driving a big car on a boat. It was too much for her brain to process. She thought about walking to the bed and breakfast and being trapped on an island four four days without a car and wondered which scenario was worse. Even if she had a car, what was she going to do? Drive along the bottom of the ocean until she came out on the other side? No, a car would not make sense. Parking in a parking lot for four days made her nervous as well, but she looked at her Teal Blue 2003 Saturn Ion and realized that if someone was going to steal a car, her car was not the one to take.

Joanie thought about the islanders and wondered what she should pack. She wanted to fit in and not look like a tourist because that was the whole point of her assignment. She had been studying Block Island maps in her travel guide for days because the last thing she wanted to do was pull out her book while trying to figure out how to get from point A to point B. She packed her bathing suit and towel because people go to the beach and packed a pair of sneakers because she assumed a bicycle would be her main mode of transportation. Joanie hadn't ridden a bicycle since she was fourteen, so she packed a helmet just in case.

There were so many items she didn't already have that she needed for this trip. She bought new sneakers, sheets and a pillow for her bed, a bathing suit, and a new backpack for whatever day trips she found herself on. Joanie didn't trust other people's sheets and pillows. She used to stay up late at night watching YouTube videos on science topics and one topic that especially freaked her out was on the dust mites and bugs that lived in your bedding. She also upgraded her cell phone service because she had no idea how good the wi-fi or cell service was and didn't want to go over her data usage. After that costly trip to SuperMart, Joanie decided to open up a separate bank account to track all her expenses.

She couldn't believe she was leaving in forty-eight hours! She met Maria and Chris for a celebratory dinner that night because this assignment was going to be amazing!

Joanie's parents retired in Florida, so she sent them a text to let them know she was leaving on Tuesday. She occasionally texted them to let them know what was going on in her life but they were busy living their best retired life. They rarely got back to her beyond the obligatory, "Great!" or random heart emojis, so Joanie wasn't expecting anything in return.

Joanie was invited to the office on Monday for a luncheon organized by Mark to send her off. She drove to the office with extra pep in her step and a big smile across her face. She never would have volunteered for this opportunity but it was placed in her lap and she couldn't help but be excited by all the unknowns.

When she walked into the office, it was eerily quiet. People were there but they weren't exactly working. They were mingling around the water cooler, standing in the cubicles, or quietly talking amongst themselves. Joanie smiled brightly and waved. Her office mate, Rebecca, waved back but didn't return the smile. Joanie looked around and found a table spread of sandwiches, donuts, juice, coffee, tea, and picnic salads. Nothing had been touched yet. There were balloons floating along the ceiling and streamers draped along the door frames. "Where is Mark?" Joanie asked Rebecca. She motioned in the direction of his office.

"Joanie! Hello!" Mark greeted her as she approached his office.

"Hi Mark. What is going on? Everyone is acting as if someone died out there."

"Oh, that. Yes. Well," Mark started but couldn't quite finish. He shoved an envelope containing a transfer slip toward her and said, "Here you go. This is for you. I just transferred some money into your account. Keep your receipts and please try not to spend it all at once. It is a 500 dollar cash advance. That should be enough to get you started. Everything else is reimbursable" Joanie took the envelope and placed it in her wallet. "Okay," he continued, "Let's go eat!"

# An Unfinished Story

    Joanie and Mark approached the table as he tried to get everyone's attention, "Ahh-hem!" He clapped his hands loudly over his head. Everyone turned and waited for his announcement. "I would like to thank Joanie for taking on this assignment to write about life on Block Island. We are going to miss having her here at the office on a daily basis but know that she will still be here, ready and willing to keep the Lifestyle section afloat. If you have any questions throughout the week, please do not hesitate to contact myself or Mikayla. Joanie may or may not have cell phone service. Please enjoy this luncheon on behalf of the office to wish Joanie the best of luck. Cheers." Mark raised his cup as if he was giving her a toast at her wedding. Everyone continued to mumble under their breaths and before the glasses were placed back on the table Mark was back in his office.
    "What's going on?" Joanie asked Mikayla. "Everyone seems ...worried." Mikayla shrugged her shoulders. "It's just the threat of everyone losing their job in a few months. I think people are ready to jump ship. I have gotten so many emails from other magazines and newspapers asking if people work here. I think they are just worried that in a few months they are going to be jobless." Joanie thought about that. Here she was, going to a vacation destination, when really, she should be looking for a job. She kind of just assumed that her job would be absorbed into whatever happened with the company. Whether the company survived or was bought out, Joanie assumed that she would still be here. Maybe she should have been a little more aware of the what-ifs.

# Chapter 5

Carly was scrambling around the foyer making sure everything was ready for the guests coming in for the weekend. Her bed and breakfast had four guest rooms and four ensuites, plus her in-law apartment off the kitchen. She found it really hard to keep the decor of the bed and breakfast completely neutral and lacking any personality. Looking around the room, no one would know if a woman or a man lived here. When her parents were actively running The Willowside, the decor was straight out of the Victorian-era. Now that Carly was in charge, the decor was straight out of IKEA. Clean lines, a modern feel, and a pop of color here and there brought the house to life. She was hoping that the modern decor would attract a younger crowd.

Carly scanned the room one more time and carried the old, expired magazines into the kitchen and dropped them into the trash bin. She sat at the kitchen table with a hot cup of tea and waited for the doorbell to ring. Today she was expecting three new couples. Two were staying until Sunday and one was staying until Monday. One room was already occupied by a family of three who came to Block Island for a wedding and decided to turn it into a vacation. They were leaving Wednesday. Today was the day that Joanie was coming. Carly thought the carriage house looked fairly clean and welcoming. She had been communicating with Chris all week, hoping that the changes she made to the carriage house was adequate for Joanie. Carly even placed a bicycle she found in the garage outside the door so that Joanie could get around the island easily. She still wondered if she was crazy allowing someone to stay for free during the busiest time of the year.

After lunch, Carly was outside in the yard watering the flower beds. Jonah, a boy that Carly went to high school with drove up in his cab and out stepped a plain, frumpy girl in baggy jeans, a button down blouse, and sensible loafers. Her short straight hair had a bandana wrapped around the perimeter of her head. She walked toward Carly carrying a backpack and a weekender bag, stuck out her hand, and said, "Hi, I'm Joanie." Carly returned the handshake and noticed the clamminess to her palm. Carly wiped her palm on her jeans and introduced herself. They walked to the carriage house so Joanie could drop off her stuff.

Joanie didn't say much. She didn't make eye contact. She didn't share any information about herself. Carly let her into the guest house and told her she would check in with her in a few hours to see if she needed anything. Carly thought about Chris and how he made it seem like this would be a great idea. Now, here she was with a person who couldn't even look at her, let alone hold a conversation. Carly wasn't trying to freak herself out, but this was definitely not what she had anticipated. She was hoping for someone like her: friendly, talkative, enthusiastic, and personable. Instead she got someone introverted, quiet, and maybe, if Carly really thought about it, rude. Joanie did say thank you but it definitely didn't seem genuine, Carly thought bitterly.

Carly emailed Chris to let him know that Joanie arrived. She needed to be careful with what she said and how she said it because Chris was dating her sister so any negativity could easily get back to Joanie. Carly knew that Joanie's purpose was to immerse herself in island life, but with her social skills, Carly had a feeling it would be difficult. Carly decided to give her the benefit of the doubt and help her however she could. Maybe for the next few days she would be Joanie's tour guide by showing her where things were and introducing her to people within the community.

Carly walked back over to the carriage house and told Joanie that she wanted to take her around once she got settled and unpacked. Joanie came over to the bed and breakfast an hour later. They walked into town instead of riding bikes because Carly thought it would be easier to chat.

"So how was your trip?" Carly asked. They could see the ocean in the far distance and the businesses of the main drag down below.

"It was good. I didn't realize how long it would take to get here from Boston. I was up at four and got off the ferry at 12. I can't imagine doing that every few days."

Carly smiled and replied, "Well, you made it safe and sound and hopefully the next trip will be easier." After a few seconds of silence, Carly continued, "Chris told me a little bit about your work. You are a reporter? What exactly are you writing about while staying here?" Carly thought if she knew what type of articles Joanie was writing she could set her up with the right people. There are less than 1,000 year round islanders and thousands and thousands of tourists every summer. If Joanie didn't know who to look for, she could be chatting up with tourists all summer long.

Joanie thought for a moment before responding. "I am writing one article a week about life on the island. I was hoping to focus on one area of island life per week. Maybe interview a few people, get to know the ins and outs of the industry, and throw in my own impression of living on Block Island." There was an awkward pause and Joanie quickly added, "Thank you for the room. That really saved me!"

"No problem." Carly thought about the different "industries" Joanie mentioned. "You could definitely interview me. I work year round and winter is completely different than summer. I could represent the hospitality job. I can introduce you to everyone on the main drag and maybe you could interview a small business owner. My second cousin is on the police force. Maybe I can see if he is available. And my dad's best friends' kids are still local fishermen. How many articles do you have to write?"

## An Unfinished Story

"Six," Joanie said. "The first week will be about my transition here and the last

week will be a wrap up. Is there a teacher I can interview? Also, I was thinking I could chat with a local farmer...if there is one."

As they entered the fish and chips shop, they had a plan. Carly had some work to do to set up all these interviews. To buy some time, they decided Joanie would attack the hospitality section first. She wanted Joanie to feel successful and felt that having a willing, open interviewee, such as herself, would start her on the right foot.

When they got home from their walk, Carly made some phone calls. She decided the best way for Joanie to meet everyone was to have everyone over. It definitely could be tricky to host people when there were guests staying at the house and when she had to juggle her mother's visits. The Willowside sat on two acres of land and the carriage house was set back from the main house so entertaining people behind the carriage house would probably be fine. They probably would be so far away that the guests wouldn't even know people were over.

Carly knew that Joanie was heading back next Tuesday and she needed her first article done for Friday. She contacted everyone on Joanie's wishlist and invited them over Sunday evening for a bonfire and hamburgers and dogs. This way every guest would be checked in and accounted for before she focused on the party.

\*\*\*\*\*\*\*\*\*\*\*\*\*\*\*\*\*\*\*\*\*\*\*\*\*\*\*\*\*\*\*\*\*\*\*\*\*\*\*\*\*\*\*\*\*\*\*\*\*\*\*\*\*\*\*\*\*\*\*\*\*\*\*\*\*\*\*\*\*\*\*
\*\*\*\*\*\*\*\*\*\*\*\*\*\*\*\*\*\*\*\*\*\*\*\*\*\*\*\*\*\*

Joanie sat on the oversized floral couch and stretched out her legs. She hadn't walked that far since college and her body was silently screaming at her. She sipped some lemonade and looked around the room. The carriage house definitely needed some love but she wasn't picky. The kitchen was olive green with formica countertops and a vinyl floor.

The floor was cracked and faded and peeling in the corners. The rug was stained from too many years of neglect and bare spots emerged at the front door.

Despite the old fixtures, the decorations themselves were new. Joanie could tell that Carly spent some time updating the place for her visit. The blanket on the bed had a chevron design and the sheets, blankets, and curtains all matched. The bathroom had new rugs and matched the shower curtain and sink accessories. Joanie wasn't going to complain because a free room was worth the confusing decor. It was obvious Carly cleaned the place, and for that, Joanie was thankful.

She texted Mark and let him know she arrived safely and what the plan was for the next few weeks. She was heading back to town next Tuesday and requested a meeting on Wednesday to discuss her plans further. She then set up a meeting with her team next Thursday to review the weekend Lifestyle section. Everything had to be ready by Friday for printing.

Mark sent her back one word: *Okay*. Joanie looked at her phone, waiting. Okay? That was all he had to say? Usually when he responded with one word it meant that he was busy or distracted, but he always told her what was interfering with their conversation. He might have said, "Hey, so and so is on the phone. Text you later." This time all she got was "Okay." She blamed it on the cell service at Block Island. Thankfully the island was close enough to the coast of Rhode Island so the cell waves could travel, but the quality of the cell waves might be deteriorating. She made a note to ask Carly when she saw her again.

Joanie sat outside the carriage house and paid attention to her senses. The sky was blue with few clouds, the grass was green, the beach was rocky and had lots of cliffs, and the only sounds filling the space were birds chirping. There were a handful of cars roaming around the island but most people biked or walked. Joanie pulled out her notebook and wrote down the occupations of the people she was hoping

## An Unfinished Story

to interview. She wrote down what little info she had about each of them. This background knowledge would help her during the cook out when she was overwhelmed by strangers and unsure what to say. Attached to her notebook was a calendar that Joanie needed to set up the interviews. She had already blocked out the boxes when she would be returning home to Boston. Her calendar was half empty and half blocked. Not a bad summer, Joanie thought to herself.

She kind of missed the hustle and bustle of city life. The quiet made her uneasy and Joanie's thoughts filled the void. If she were home right now, she would be sitting in front of her television catching up on HGTV shows. Even if she wasn't watching it, the background noise would push her along to get things done. There was no television in the carriage house, which added to the authenticity of island life. When you are surrounded by peace, beauty, and tranquility, do you really need a television to distract your days? Probably not.

When Joanie was a kid, her parents took her and her sister to Cape Cod on vacation. Joanie and Maria would venture out of the beach house to the sand and build elaborate sand villages equipped with characters. Included in their beach toys were dolls and animals that would make their world come to life. Maria was eighteen months younger than Joanie but most strangers would assume they were twins. They both had light, curly hair as children, deep chestnut eyes, and fair freckled skin. Maria didn't know it, but Joanie would follow her lead when it came to playing with other kids and talking to others. Joanie never knew what to say and she always felt silly. Maria was the outgoing, mischievous one while Joanie was the quiet, introspective one. Joanie always wanted to be more like Maria.

When high school hit, everyone knew Maria. The smart kids, the jocks, the stoners, the musicians, and all the teachers knew her name. Joanie became known as "Maria's sister" and Joanie often felt forgotten even though she was older and had been through the school first. No matter how hard she tried, she was constantly within her sister's shadow. She borrowed Maria's clothes without asking, had Maria do her hair and makeup for dances, and tagged along to the movies with Maria and her friends on Friday nights. As they got older, the gap between them widened and now they barely talked. Maria lived in Newport, Rhode Island, which really was not far from Boston. Newport was a posh city that was draped in beautiful architecture and beautiful scenery. Her boyfriend, Chris, worked for a construction company, and Maria managed a high end jewelry store right on the water. It wasn't what Joanie would ever want, but it was definitely appropriate for Maria's personality.

It was ironic how little the two women spoke, yet they were logistically so close to each other and so close in age. Driving home to Boston, Joanie could easily drive through Newport. She had to thank Chris for setting her up with housing this summer, right? Joanie pulled out her cell phone and texted Maria asking if she would be around on Tuesday. It had been about a year since they had last seen each other. Her parents always talked about how the two girls were the only thing they would eventually have. No one knows you like your sister, her mother would always say. Joanie hoped Maria would respond. It really had been too long.

Joanie hopped on her bike and started riding. She carried her notebook and pencil in the basket in front of the bike and decided to go get lost. When she was a kid, she rode her bike all through their old neighborhood, hoping to get lost. Instead of getting scared, her imagination took over and she was transported into a world of curiosity and mystery. She always made her way back home, even without the aid of a cell phone, and her mother never knew that she created an alternate universe where she often lived. Joanie knew she wouldn't really get lost because of technology and cell phones today, but she thought that if she fell off the beaten path, her observations would create an authenticity to her writing that would help sell newspapers.

## An Unfinished Story

The scenery was beautiful. The green hills, isolated homes within the hills, and rocky cliffs transported Joanie to a majestic land. She rode into town, through the touristy crowds and out the other side. She rode along the beach and watched the sun fall into the ocean. The oranges, reds, and pinks filled the sky and reflected off the calm blue of the waves. Joanie kept going. The island itself was only seven miles long. Although she would get tired, there was no way she would get lost.

Once she left the downtown strip, she quickly ended up in a remote part of the island. Less cars, less people, and the random stray dog shared the narrow, windy road toward the beach. Joanie pulled her bike to the side of the road and hiked down to the beach. She sat on the beige sand and looked out at the ocean. She listened to the waves lap against the rocks, saw the birds circling the water looking for food, and smelled the salt that saturated her nose. It truly was beautiful and peaceful. Joanie knew she had to be chatty, friendly, and social during the cook-out this weekend. She could feel the anxiety growing in her chest and traveling up the back of her throat. She told herself it was only a few hours of her life and she would be fine. Joanie closed her eyes and focused on her five senses. For now, she was just going to watch the sun slowly set and focus on the moment. The beauty surrounding her calmed her nerves.

# Chapter 6

Carly ran around the kitchen collecting all the condiments. Ketchup, mustard, relish, mayonnaise, plastic utensils, paper plates, napkins and a napkin holder filled her arms as she nudged the screen door open with her hip. She reached out to everyone on her list and invited them over for an early cookout. It was certainly a bizarre group of people. Carly knew some of them well and some of them not so well. Thankfully, they all agreed to come, even the few who only knew her name and her business.

Her second cousin, Joe Murphy, certainly wasn't surprised to hear from her. He usually stopped over at the B and B to make sure her smoke alarms and carbon monoxide detectors were working. He was Carly's age and had left the island after high school. He moved to the mainland to attend the Rhode Island Police Academy. Carly remembered how heartbroken his parents were when he left, because although everyone returned at some point, many tried their hardest to stay away from island life. Joe had a bit of culture shock when he left. He suddenly could drive wherever he wanted whenever he wanted. He didn't have to check the ferry schedule. He could stop at a coffee shop and not run into anyone familiar. It was a wonderful break from reality but always left him feeling uneasy. Joe graduated with Honors from the police academy and got a job as a patrolman in Providence. After a few years, he returned home. He lived at his parents house, helping them tend to the property and eventually obtained a job working for the police department. Vacancies were few and far between because the population was small and crime was

## An Unfinished Story

low. Officers never retired, but when they did, the department struggled with finding a qualified applicant. Joe fell into a position less than a year after returning home. His parents both passed away and their property was passed down to Joe. This type of transaction was common on Block Island because families that settled there originally passed down their property from generation to generation.

Lucas and Logan Brown were coming to the cookout also. Their father, Michael, was the local fisherman who delivered to all the eating establishments on the island. He would deliver to The Willowside weekly with fresh fish. During Lent, Carly's Catholic family would not eat meat and Michael would drop off whatever fish he had leftover after the local deliveries free of charge for her family. Michael was a little younger than Carly's father, and Carly's father always wanted a son. They became fast friends and Michael taught Carly's father how to fish. Michael had passed away, but he taught his two sons how to catch fish and run a business. They still had relationships with all the businesses on the island. When tourism was down or when it was offseason, they continued to deliver to locals. Carly didn't know Logan and Lucas as well as Michael, but she thought that they would be able to give Joanie enough factual and anecdotal information about life as fishermen to write an entertaining article.

Mrs. Stanley was Carly's teacher during all four high school years. Schooling was strange here because there were so few kids the entire school was mixed into just a few classrooms. Each student got the same coursework, but maybe not during the same year of education. This was the most cost effective way of running the school. Carly graduated with a class of nine and her entire high school had forty five kids. Carly dreamed of living somewhere else, where you could make stupid mistakes without being reminded of it by every single person you passed.

Mrs. Stanley was one of two teachers in her high school years (if you could even call it that). She was now in her seventies and still working. Carly wasn't sure how effective her teaching was because she had become terribly hard of hearing as the years continued. It was weird to think that when Carly graduated from high school, those same children born that year had the same teacher Carly did. Mrs. Stanley was surprised to hear from Carly, especially since Carly didn't have any kids of her own within the school system, but she loved to connect with old students and see what they were up to.

The most uncomfortable exchange was with the beekeepers, Andrew and Sara Cohen. The Cohen's inherited some land from a great aunt and moved to Block Island about four years prior from upstate New York. In New York, they took care of beehives and processed and sold honey for farmer's markets. They were in their thirties and did not have any children so they ventured to Block Island where they would live mortgage free. Thankfully, the property they inherited was on six acres, which was plenty of room to set up their beehives. The Cohen's had a store downtown selling honey, but they also traveled to the mainland to expand their name at various farmer's markets. Carly thought it would be good for Joanie to get some perspective from an outsider trying to live on Block Island.

When Carly called, the Cohen's had no idea who she was or why she was calling. Carly loved to talk to people in person, but really struggled with telephone exchanges because body language and facial expressions were absent. Those things really helped Carly decipher the meaning behind their words. Carly stumbled over her words and her explanation, but finally was able to get her point across. Sara agreed to come over and volunteered to bring some delicious honey. Carly couldn't wait to incorporate their honey into her cooking.

Carly set up a plastic table and placed a vinyl pineapple tablecloth on it and waited for everyone to arrive. Joanie was inside prepping all the food and drinks. They decided that having the food mostly inside would be best, just in case the weather shifted, as it often did. Joanie thanked Carly for doing this, but Carly could tell that Joanie was uncomfortable. She

# An Unfinished Story

seemed to be trying to keep busy and trying to be helpful with the setup, but was talking quickly, asking a lot of questions, and forgetting to actually do what Carly asked of her. Joanie admitted that she struggled with meeting new people and Carly wondered how she even got into journalism if she was afraid to talk to people.

Carly extended the invitation to the guests at The Willowside that weekend. Although they were just visitors, she thought it would have been rude to not include them. Plus, if Joanie truly did struggle with small talk, then maybe the guests would be a good buffer. They didn't know anyone either, and maybe through conversation, Joanie would pick up on some information to ask more questions to the locals. The three sets of guests were already outside, drinks in hand, sitting around the empty fire pit chatting about where they wanted to go or what they wanted to see during their vacation.

Ding! Carly ran to the door to find the Cohen's, of all people, first to arrive. "Hello! Welcome!" she exclaimed.

"Hi Carly! Thank you for inviting us! We brought you some honey. It tastes delicious with pita chips! We were wondering if you could put some out for everyone to try?" Sarah pushed a jar of honey into Carly's chest.

Carly smiled and said, "Of course! Follow me into the kitchen." As she poured the honey into a small bowl, she introduced Sarah and Andrew to Joanie. Joanie stuck out her hand, and said, "Hello! My name is Joanie. It is so nice to meet you!" The Cohen's tried to engage in small talk, but Joanie just responded with short answers that really didn't help anyone expand on their topic of conversation. After an awkward pause, Carly jumped in and explained why Joanie was on the island. Joanie smiled and followed the Cohen's into the yard. Her shoulders were tense and her gait was stiff. Carly knew she felt uncomfortable just being there.

All the other guests trickled in slowly. Some brought side dishes or dessert and some came empty handed. Once the food was out, Carly looked out the kitchen window at the random group of people she assembled. Some islanders, some visitors, and one reporter who had a notebook and pen ready to jot down any pertinent information that came up in conversation were milling around the firepit. Carly thought she should go out there and help Joanie, but decided that she would just watch everything unfold. She was doing Joanie a favor just having this random group of people together. Joanie was here because she had a job to do, and it sounded like Joanie had been doing this job for years. Yes, Carly thought, she definitely knew what she was doing.

*******************************************************************
**********************************

The number of people was overwhelming but Joanie knew that time was not on her side and she had a deadline. She took a deep breath and approached a man, who looked to be in his mid forties. He had short, dark, wavy hair and a beard that was speckled with white. His face certainly wasn't wrinkled, but it definitely was lined from worry. "How is the dip?" Joanie asked, nodding her head toward the plate he was holding.

The man turned to face her and eyed her up and down. "Good," he replied.

Joanie waited for more, but nothing else came. "Today is a beautiful day," she said, raising her eyes toward the sky.

"Sure is," the man replied.

Joanie waited again. Nothing. This conversation-thing was going to be harder than she thought. "My name is Joanie. I am staying in Carly's guest house for a few weeks," she introduced herself and stuck out her hand. The man took it and introduced himself as Joe. He explained that he was related to Carly and worked for the police force.

Joanie gave him her biggest smile and told him she was writing weekly articles for the Boston Tribune about Island LIfe. "I would love to sit down with you over a cup of coffee and talk about your experiences!"

They awkwardly chatted about the job, the crime, the gratitude of the locals, and the challenges island life

## An Unfinished Story

presented. Joanie couldn't help but notice his dark hair, healthy build, and blue eyes. She couldn't help but notice that one dimple appeared every time he smiled. She couldn't help but notice the way his brow furrowed when he was thinking. The awkwardness was partly because Joanie didn't really know much about being a police officer on an island and she was leading the conversation, but partly because looking at Joe was distracting and causing her thoughts to jumble.

Joanie looked down at her notes and realized that she only had enough information for half her required word count. She was digging for information. "So, how often do people stay in the workforce?", "Do you ever have people apply and get hired from the mainland?", "What is the scariest situation you have ever been put in?" were questions she asked. She was interested in the ins-and-outs of the job, but more interested in the anecdotal stories Joe told. The stories Joe told allowed her to look into his soul without being too forward.

"Excuse me," a man tapped her on the shoulder. He was one of the guests staying at the house. "Do you have any more honey? It tastes delicious with these chips," the man held out an empty bowl with a coating of stickiness at the bottom.

"Absolutely!" Joanie exclaimed with a grin on her face. She was getting so caught up in Joe's stories that she totally forgot she needed to network with all of these people. "Excuse me," she turned to Joe and sauntered off into the kitchen hoping that he was watching her walk away. *Focus* she told herself. *Focus.* Joanie filled the bowl with honey, set it on the table, and decided to approach Mr. and Mrs. Cohen next.

Joanie internally practiced various ways to politely interrupt their conversation. *Excuse me...Hi, I'm Joanie!...That is some excellent honey!* Joanie shook her head. Maybe she should just laugh when they were laughing, she thought to herself. This is why Joanie went into business and not marketing or journalism. Talking to people was just too hard for her to manage.

"Your honey is delicious! All the guests agree," Joanie blurted to the couple. They turned toward her and smiled.

"Thank you. It's organic and home grown." Sara responded.

"I would love to buy some off of you. It is delicious!" Joanie stumbled.

"Of course. I am Sara," Sara said, holding out her hand.

Joanie took her hand and shook it, realizing that the honey from the jar dripped down her fingers. She thought she wiped it off but the sticky residue remained. Sara immediately pulled away and grabbed a towel. Joanie put the Cohen's on the bottom of her list for who to contact next. She excused herself and went to the bathroom to clean her hands.

Next, Joanie approached Mrs. Stanley. Mrs. Stanley's white curly hair was blowing in the breeze. It appeared she had gotten her hair set that day. She was sitting near the fire alone and quietly observing the guests. Joanie sat next to her and said hello. Mrs. Stanly didn't turn her head or acknowledge her. Joanie didn't know what to do. She cleared her throat and said hello louder. Still no response. She knew she looked like a crazy person talking to herself with an animated smile on her face to anyone who was observing her. She heard a quiet voice behind her say, "She can't hear you." Joanie turned to find Joe grinning from ear to ear.

Joanie rose so her back was facing Mrs. Stanley and whispered, "Thank you! I was about to get up and tap her on the shoulder!"

"Hey Joe!" a young man with blonde, wavy hair approached them. Mrs. Stanley turned and smiled and the young man waved. He turned to Joe and said, "Do you need any bass? We have a catch that no one has ordered if you need some."

"Logan, this is Joanie. Have you met?" When Logan shook his head, Joe said, "Joanie, this is Logan." They smiled and shook hands professionally. Logan seemed friendly with kind eyes and a gentle smile. He seemed to share his fish,

# An Unfinished Story

which was neighborly of him. Joanie decided she would interview him after Joe.

They chatted back and forth talking about the seas and the weather and the type of fish common to Block Island. Joanie asked if they could meet up for coffee sometime so she could work on her articles. They exchanged numbers and made a tentative date for the next weekend.

Joanie continued to roam around the group, listening in on conversations, helping Carly refill food and drinks, and then cleaning up once all the guests left. She couldn't thank Carly enough for throwing this gathering together. Although she didn't hit it off with everyone, she did feel like the ice was broken, which would make the next contact just a little bit easier.

Carly smiled and told Joanie that she would help her get ready for the interviews and coffee dates. Joanie was thankful because Carly could give her more background information to help the interview run smoothly. As long as she had some information, she could prepare her interview questions in advance.

The next day, Joanie met Joe at the only coffee shop in town to get more information about his work. She told him she needed to meet the next day because her article was due, which was a half-truth. Joanie had stayed up most of the night thinking about his strong physique, mysterious eyes, and perfectly fitting jeans.

They met for coffee and conversation happened naturally. She listened intently to his answers and inferred that he was single, he liked his job, and he and Carly had frequent communication. Joanie knew that he came around The Willowside every few weeks, he worked the second and third shift, and he was living on his family property. Joanie drank her coffee quickly and asked the waitress for a refill. She didn't want the conversation to end. Joe looked at his watch and commented that he had to get to work.

Joanie sat at the table with her full cup of coffee as Joe excused himself. They didn't discuss seeing each other again, which disappointed Joanie. She assumed that he only met with her for the purpose of completing her article and she accepted that she might not ever see him again. On an impulse that Joanie had no control over, she grabbed the pen the waitress had left on the table and touched Joe's arm to get his attention. Her body stiffened up and she felt his arm tense at her touch. They locked eyes and Joanie started fumbling. "Um, I, uh, I was wondering if we could exchange numbers." She felt a warmth run up her neck to her forehead and smiled nervously. "Just in case there was any information I still needed to verify or add," she added. "Or if you wanted to share some other information with me you can." Her eyes fell to the table, not quite sure how he would interpret that last sentence. He hesitated and then quickly wrote down his number on a napkin and she did the same. She shoved it into her bag and they said good-bye.

Joanie eventually made her way back to the carriage house. Tomorrow was Tuesday and she was heading back to Boston. Wednesday and Thursday she had a meeting set up with Mark and with her team to make sure that the Lifestyle section was ready for printing on Saturday. She hadn't even written her first article because she was so wrapped up in making sure the rest of her articles were possible.

Joanie pulled out her laptop, sat in the wicker chair on the front porch, and started writing about her experiences coming to a small island off the coast of Rhode Island. She decided to format her article like a journal entry so she could connect to her readers on a personal level. She would write about the community of people, the scenery, where she was living, and how her first week unfolded. She hoped her personality shone through the words and pulled her readers in enough that they would want to buy another paper just to see what happened next.

# Chapter 7

Joanie walked into the office. The office was abuzz with chatter and people moving from cubicle to cubicle. Phones were ringing, papers rustling, and computers were pinging with notifications that emails were received. The sun was shining brightly through the open blinds and the shadows of people walking danced along the floor.

"How is everything?" Joanie asked Marley, the woman next to her desk. "It seems like a big story just broke." Joanie looked around the room and tried to read facial expressions. Everyone seemed tense as they moved around the room.

"Geez, Joanie! Do you not watch the news?" Joanie didn't have time to watch the news. She had just returned from a place with no cable. She was lucky if she got local weather, let alone actual news. She arrived late last night after visiting her sister. She completely crashed while watching Netflix and woke up with a start to hear her alarm buzzing. No, she didn't see the news.

Joanie turned on her phone. She didn't have any text messages from anyone important. Nothing from Mark and she was supposed to be meeting him in 10 minutes. "No, actually I haven't. What's up?" Marley raised her eyebrows as if to say, *What a great manager you are!* She pulled up the local news station on her computer. On the homepage, in big letters, it read, *Boston Paper Bought out by Chicago Media Giant.* "Oh shit," Joanie mumbled under her breath. She quickly scanned the article but little information was given. Boston Tribune struggling for years. Chicago Globe purchased local paper for 2.1 million dollars. As of August

## An Unfinished Story

1st, Boston Tribune will be run by Chicago Globe. That was all it said.

Joanie frantically looked around the room. "Where is Mark?" Her eyes narrowed as she recognized his dark office. He wasn't there.

"I don't know. We haven't seen or heard from him at all." Marley responded. She sat at her desk and sighed heavily. Marley picked up the picture of herself, her husband, and her two small children and turned it upside down. "What am I going to do if I lose my job?" Marley placed her head in her hands. Joanie felt safe from the transition because she was a manager, but Marley was just a first level associate. She took care of the classifieds, which most people didn't even use anymore. Joanie agreed that her position would probably be eliminated.

"Don't worry Marley. Until we talk to Mark, we really don't know what is going to happen." Joanie pulled out her phone and texted Mark. *Mark, call me. The office is a mess. I need to know what is going on. Where are you?* She hit send and waited. Just a blank screen stared back at her. She put her phone face up on her desk and turned the silence function off.

She opened her email searching for clues. Nothing. She pulled up Google and searched: Boston Tribune sold. A list of articles opened but none of them gave any specific information. One report stated that the paper could lose up to 70% of its workforce. The only good thing, thought Joanie, was that the new owner was out of Chicago, so it was unlikely that all their jobs would be replaced. Joanie started laughing to herself. Her quiet chuckles turned into giggles which turned into cackles which turned into sobs. She didn't care that people in the office stopped and looked to see what was wrong or what was so funny. The irony that they, a media company, were not notified of the sale of their own company until other media companies reported the sale. It was hysterically sad. She felt like all their credibility was gone.

As Joanie tried to sort through her thoughts, people kept approaching her with questions: August 1st is only five weeks away. When will they be notified if they still have a job? How will this affect retirement? Should they keep working on their assignments? Where was Mark? Joanie had no idea how to answer their questions, so she just smiled and said, "Mark will be here soon." She had no idea if or when he would show up. She had no idea why he wouldn't be here holding the fort together when the news broke. He blew off her meeting with him, which was not like him at all. Joanie suggested they continue working as if it were just another day. She suggested they email her their questions and promised the anxious staff that when she met with Mark she would ask him the questions on their behalf.

Joanie knew nothing would get done today. There was no way people would be able to work as if nothing were happening. Most of these people (herself included) lived paycheck to paycheck. Joanie kept telling everyone not to worry until there was something to worry about. It was easier said than done and she knew that most of them were searching and applying for new jobs because the potential outcome of the news was too much to consider.

Throughout the day, Joanie checked her phone, but no messages were waiting for her. She checked her watch, her phone, and her email repeatedly. She had eighty-eight new emails that were intended for Mark. She knew she should be reading and jotting down concerns for her friends and colleagues, but the responsibility was too much for her. She looked in her purse for change so she could grab a candy bar from the vending machine. She looked around the room and saw that no one was working. She looked at her watch again. She had two more hours to go and knew if she left and showed defeat, the entire office would also leave and feel defeated. She knew if they left defeated they might never return. They need each other and Joanie wouldn't allowe herself to be the one who set the resignation ball rolling. She couldn't do that. So instead, she continued to google, research, and check emails. By the end of the day, there was still nothing from Mark.

# An Unfinished Story

*******************************************************************
******************************

    Carly hopped on the ferry with an overnight bag in hand. The bag was filled with clean laundry to drop off at her mom's facility. Every Wednesday, Carly made the trek into the mainland to check in on her mom. They usually visited for a few hours. Carly ate lunch with her mom, put her clothes away, picked up her dirty clothes, and watched the news with her. Sometimes her mom knew who she was and other times, it was like they had just met for the first time. When her mom was confused by Carly's presence, Carly often played along praying that her mom wouldn't snap into a lucid moment and then be hurt by the charade Carly played with her. This had happened on more than one occasion, but when Carly tried to correct her mom's confusion, her mom became agitated and combative. Either situation resulted in her mom feeling hurt, but Carly would rather have her feel mocked than angry. Usually when her mom realized Carly was pretending to be someone else, she ended up feeling mocked and angry. It was a situation Carly could never win.

    Carly looked out at the blue waves. She stood on the top deck of the ferry and breathed in the salty air. The wind pushed her hair back, which allowed the sun to beat down on her fair skin. The hour ride allowed Carly a time to reflect on the past week, month, year, and life. She knew she would one day have to care for her parents but she never realized how much of a sacrifice in time and money it would be. Thankfully, the inn did not accept new patrons on Wednesdays, which allowed a day for the cleaning woman to come in and upkeep the bed and breakfast. Carly was grateful that she could see her mom and not feel guilty about neglecting her business.

    The ferry was heading to New London, CT, which was a much bigger city than the small towns that dotted the Rhode Island coast. Carly did not take a car on the ferry because the expense was exorbitant. On a nice day, she was able to walk to the nursing home which overlooked the ocean. If her mother was in a facility inland, she would be miserable. The ocean was what kept her grounded throughout her life. Carly was even able to coordinate a room for a little extra money with a window facing the ocean. When her mother was in a lucid state, they were able to sit outside and watch the waves lap against the coast.

Carly exited the ferry and walked down the bustling streets that ran parallel to the Long Island Sound. Even though it was practically July, the humidity broke and a nice breeze pushed her along to London Rehab. Carly signed in and knocked on her mom's door. It was 10:45, which was the usual time she arrived. A nurse was in the room taking her vitals and trying to convince her to swallow her crushed pills. Carly's mom hated applesauce. *They had to figure out a better way*, Carly thought to herself.

"Hi Mom!" Carly cheerfully exclaimed, dropping the overnight bag on a chair. She bent down and gave her mom a kiss. Carly's mom smiled up at her as the nurse shoved the spoon in her mouth and gave her a glass of water to wash it down. In the past, her mother had been known to spit out the applesauce. Carly was thankful that today was not one of those days.

"Carly!" Carly was relieved that her mother recognized her. Sometimes she would look at Carly with blank eyes. When Ruth looked at her with a blank stare, Carly felt completely disconnected and felt like she didn't belong there. It always made her sad because she only visited once a week and when the visits weren't good, it seemed like such a waste.

"How is she?" Carly asked the nurse before she scurried out of the room.

"Good. We switched her meds last night because she has been having difficulty sleeping. We will know if it is a good fit by Friday. She is probably tired. Lately she has been napping around 1, which might be why she isn't sleeping well at night." Carly nodded, looking to her beautiful mom, as the nurse left the room. It was hard watching her mother get old and sick.

## An Unfinished Story

Carly used to feel resentful that her parents were so old when she was born, but Carly realized just how short life can be and how quickly things can change.

"How are you feeling, Mom?" Carly asked.

"Good, good," her mother replied. Lately, conversation was hard to maintain. Even though they didn't say much, Carly knew her mom was grateful for the company. Every now and then her mom reached to the chair Carly was sitting in and stroked her arm without saying a word.

"I brought your clothes." Carly unpacked and hung up the clothes in the bag and placed the dirty clothes in the overnight bag to wash at home. She also snuck a small unwrapped Hershey's chocolate bar to her mother. It was Ruth's favorite candy and sneaking chocolate became somewhat of a tradition.

Carly wheeled Ruth outside into the warm, bright sunshine. They sat in silence and took in the environment. The warm sun, the birds flying above, the buzzing of bees, the lapping of the waves, and the quiet conversation of those around them put Carly at ease. Carly arranged lunch to be outside and they ate in silence.

Although conversation was limited, Carly shared what was going on in her life. Stories of her new houseguest, the cookout, the newspaper assignment, and her shopping excursion to brighten up the carriage house monopolized the lunch conversation. Her mom just smiled and nodded and said, "mmm," when Carly showed her pictures. She tried to take pictures on her phone often to help stir up some memories for her mom. She thought maybe seeing the carriage house would trigger a memory or seeing the most recent sunset would trigger a story about better days but it never did.

After lunch Carly wheeled her mom back into her room for a nap. She looked tired. Carly placed a throw over her mom's shoulders, put whatever talk show was on on the small television, and kissed her on the cheek. "Bye mom, I will see you next week. Thanks for having lunch with me." Her mom smiled and turned her attention to the television. Carly grabbed the overnight back and headed to the ferry. *Just another day in the life of caring for your elderly parents*, she thought to herself.

*********************************************************************************

The hot sun beat down on Joanie's back as she walked to her car. The humidity was stifling and she found it difficult to breathe. She had so many thoughts running through her head. It was like her thoughts were competing with each other to gain her attention and were bumping into each other and ricocheting off her skull. She dug into her bag and pulled out the travel sized bottle of Advil.

What was she going to do? Where was Mark? Should she continue working on her assignment? Should she be looking for other jobs? The number of unknowns was overwhelming. Joanie texted Mark again and reviewed the message history. She had sent seven text messages of increasing urgency over the past week and none of them had been acknowledged. She didn't want to go back to the island and she didn't want to stay at home. If she stayed at home, she would sit on her couch alone, pretending to watch television, and actually running her mind off a cliff with all the what-ifs.

Joanie climbed into her car and threw her work bag onto the passenger seat. Her dash started beeping at her because it thought her passenger forgot to put on a seatbelt. She reached over and threw her bag on the floor of the car. Instead of going home, Joanie decided to drive by Mark's house. If he was home, she was going to knock on his door and demand answers. If he wasn't home, she was going to leave a note on his door begging for communication.

Traffic was atrocious. Mark lived further into the city, which required special attention to all the merges, unfamiliar potholes, and random rotaries located in overcrowded towns and cities. Joanie wasn't usually brave enough to venture into the city during rush hour, but her body wasn't communicating with her brain and all common sense had disappeared.

# An Unfinished Story

Joanie couldn't even remember exactly where he lived, but she thought maybe heading in the right direction would trigger her memories of driving over there to drop off her assignment before the bell rang and it was technically late. He was livid with her that day because she almost caused the entire Lifestyle section to not be included in the printing. How do you even explain that? Mark had asked. Do you leave out a section and hope no one notices? Do you put in old articles and hope no one notices? Do you throw in garbage that had been omitted and hope no one notices? He was red in the face, talking fast, and complaining that he was going to be up all night because it was his head on the chopping block. Joanie felt terrible that day, but her grandmother had just died. She felt that she deserved some sort of compassion. Maybe she should have told him she wasn't mentally able to handle it. Maybe he should have known. Maybe, Joanie thought to herself, this job wasn't meant for her.

As Joanie drove, her phone pinged. Frantically, and without taking her eyes off the road, she searched within her bag for her phone. *Call me.* It was from Mark! She pulled into the strip mall parking lot and called. "Mark!" she exclaimed when he answered. "Where have you been?"

"I have been on the phone all day desperately trying to figure out what is going on! Sorry I didn't respond to your calls. I didn't want to talk until I had something to say. Can you talk now?" he asked.

"Actually I was on my way over to your house. But I don't remember where you live," Joanie said sheepishly. "Do you want to grab a quick bite to eat? I am sitting in front of Starbucks. There is a 5 Guys restaurant here if you want to grab some food. I am in Medford right now." Mark told her he would be there in ten minutes and would explain everything.

Joanie sat at a pub table facing the parking lot. The table was covered in shredded lettuce and drink rings from soda cups that hadn't been consumed quick enough. She was going to wait for him before ordering but felt more comfortable taking up a table with food rather than just sitting suspiciously waiting. She ordered a lemonade to buy some time. Her lemonade was chilled, sweet, and sour all at the same time. The cool liquid felt refreshing as she swallowed. Her stomach was jumping into her chest as she saw Mark climb out of her car.

Mark scooted into the bench across from her. "Hi," he said. He was wearing a crumpled white button down shirt that either had been worn three times before today and not washed, or had just been pulled out of the hamper. He set a folder of papers on the table. He had beads of sweat formed around the perimeter of his face and his glasses slid down to the tip of his nose. He clumsily readjusted his glasses and wiped his forehead.

"Joanie. I am telling you. I had no idea. I woke up, like every other day and turned on the news while I got dressed. The story was briefly told in between the weather and sports. All it said was that we were bought out. I was shocked. So I spent the entire day calling Mr. Hill, the owner of Boston Tribune, and trying to get a hold of anyone at headquarters in Chicago. After a lot of phone tag, voicemails, and messages, I finally got through." Mark stopped and waited but no response came. He continued, "How has everyone been this week?"

"Well, you know ...nervous, afraid, and not very productive. I told them they had to have their articles in as usual, and we would make sure things went off without a hitch. I am assuming we are going to be the headline on Sunday's front page?" Joanie waited for Mark to answer but he was fumbling on his phone responding to an email. "Everyone has a lot of questions. I actually have over one hundred emails from concerned employees with questions ranging in job security to healthcare to unused vacation time. So tell me, what is going on?" Joanie asked, staring directly into his eyes. She held his gaze until he responded.

"Well, it's true. The sale of the newspaper closed yesterday. Mr. Hill didn't want it to happen so fast, but once the news came out that we were down in our quarterly report

## An Unfinished Story

and were losing money, Chicago made an offer he couldn't refuse. It's so funny that we talked about the potential crisis, not even a month ago, and now here we are. No, not funny. It's ironic, sad, and shocking. I guess by us being in Boston, it made sense for Chicago to try and broaden their scope. Now they are a media giant in Chicago with offices in Boston and LA."

Joanie sat quietly for a moment. "So what is going to happen to us?" she asked.

Mark shrugged. "I don't know. It's too soon for any definitive information. I do know that August 15th, people from headquarters will be coming in, looking at our work space, our finished products, and interviewing folks to keep their jobs. From what I gathered, September 1st will be the day we know for sure if we have a job or not." Joanie smiled behind her anxiety. September 1st. That was only six weeks away. Six weeks to prove that her position was meant to be kept and that she was the proper person to be in that position. In six weeks time, her future would be decided with very little say from her. Joanie stood up, told Mark she had to go, and went home to lose herself in reality television while eating frozen pizza and forgetting that this was happening in her real life.

The next day, at the office, people kept to themselves. There wasn't the usual laughter or gossip floating over the cubicles. Joanie closed her eyes and all she could hear was the clicking of keyboards. She wasn't sure if people were invested in their work and proving their worth, or if they were hurriedly updating their resumes. Whatever the reason was behind the eerily quiet atmosphere, Joanie was thankful that the constant noise was gone.

She printed out her article and put it with the other lifestyle reports. She liked to keep hard copies, just in case something came up at home and she didn't have access to her computer. She sent everything to the editor to arrange for Sunday's paper. Joanie packed up her bag and left for the day. It was time to head back to Carly's carriage house and figure out what she was going to do for the next article.

Erica Haraldsen

August 1st was two weeks away, and by then her life might be completely turned on its heel.

# Chapter 8

Carly flipped the bacon sizzling in the frying pan. She had three hot pots and pans on the stove. One for bacon, one for eggs, and one for pancakes. The coffee was brewing and the aroma filled the room. She closed her eyes, inhaled deeply, and then flipped and stirred everything cooking. It was 7 am and breakfast ran from 7:30-9:00 in the dining room. Today she had three of her four guest rooms full. Joanie returned late last night. Carly saw the taxi pull into the driveway at dusk. Joanie pulled out a small duffel bag and scurried into the carriage house.

Carly wasn't sure if Joanie would come for breakfast, but she knew it was always available. Carly was getting used to having a second person on the property, even if it was just a few days at a time. It was difficult for Carly to not think of Joanie as a guest because she had been serving guests for years now. She often had to resist the urge to enter the carriage house when Joanie wasn't there to clean the kitchen and change the sheets.

Carly bumped into Joe at the grocery store the other day and he asked her when Joanie was returning. Carly looked at his tall frame, dark hair, and tired eyes. She thought of his life and their relationship, and wondered how two single cousins, right around the same age, living in the same place, were practically strangers. Joe came by every few weeks but he never stayed. They were connected yet they didn't even know each other. She told Joe that Joanie came around on the weekends and would be back on Friday or Saturday. He smiled and said, "Maybe I will see you around."

## An Unfinished Story

The tea kettle started whistling and Carly was snapped back into the kitchen. She could hear the guests congregating in the dining room, helping themselves to the toast and jam station and juice station. Carly placed all the hot food in metal containers and finished setting up breakfast.

"Good Morning!" she called as she sauntered into the dining room. Six strangers at three different tables greeted her with a mix of emotion. Some smiled, some buried their noses into a newspaper, and some continued to look out the window, commenting on the wildlife outside. "Today for breakfast we have scrambled eggs, hash browns, pancakes with homemade syrup and honey from the island. Coffee, tea, and juice are over here, and toast and pastries are over here," Carly pointed to various tables around the room feeling like Vanna White. "Enjoy!" she exclaimed as she exited the dining room.

She sat at the kitchen table and picked up the paper. Block Island had its own newsletter that came out twice a month. It was basically a calendar of events and a classified section. During the spring and early summer, it was mostly classifieds, advertisements for seasonal businesses, and a calendar of festivals. Because her guests came from all over, Carly had a variety of newspapers delivered, which cost quite a bit of money, but she felt that actual newspapers that you can hold, feel, and fold, made her bed and breakfast experience much more authentic.

The Boston Tribune was one of the papers delivered every Sunday. The front page had an article about The Boston Tribune being bought out. *Wow,* Carly thought to herself, *I didn't expect to see that!* She wondered if Joanie knew and how she was feeling. She hadn't mentioned anything to her when they saw each other last week, but she did seem a little stressed. Joanie's hair was a mess and thrown up into a messy bun. She had on her running shoes and told Carly she needed to go investigate the island to get a feel for the culture. Carly didn't think anything of it, but she wondered if running was her way of dealing with life's uncertainties.

The article said that the paper was bought out by a company in Chicago that was slowly buying out small, independent papers all over the east coast. They were building their empire, apparently. The article mentioned that the transfer would occur on August 1st. Joanie looked at her calendar. August first was two weeks away. It said that all employees would be notified of their positions by August 15th. Four weeks. *That was all it took to completely change your life*, Carly thought.

She flipped through the paper, pulled out all the store advertisements, and opened up the Lifestyle Section. On the front page was Joanie's article, Island Life, and this week's story was all about Carly. Carly and The Willowside B and B was reviewed in such a positive light that Carly knew her business would soar. Joanie talked about the family history of The Willowside, the local ingredients used in her cooking, and the one of a kind location the visitors got to explore Block Island. Joanie also mentioned the difficulty juggling a seasonal business, the loneliness of living on an island during the quiet months, and the community and comradery that other locals exhibited to support one another. Carly made a note to herself to ask Joanie about the two articles when she saw her later.

*******************************************************************
*******************************

Joanie looked down at her phone. Thirty five new emails and four voicemails in three hours. She scanned through the notifications. Mark called once but didn't leave a voicemail. Her emails were mostly from co-workers panicking over their future. Joanie couldn't think straight, let alone deal with everyone else's questions and concerns. She turned her phone off, dropped it in her bag, and sat down in the patio chair outside the carriage house.

## An Unfinished Story

She closed her eyes and raised her face to the sun. The warm beams were beating on her cheeks and the cool breeze contradicted the warmth. She kept her eyes closed and allowed her mind to wander. She was annoyed at herself because thoughts of work were suffocating her. She knew she had to eventually call people back but she decided today would not be the day. She knew she had to continue on with her interviews but decided she would start tomorrow. She knew she had to look for another job but decided she would start next week.

The birds were singing a tune in the trees next to her. She watched the flowers dance in the garden. She watched the large, puffy clouds merge from one shape into the next. She listened to the music playing faintly from the house across the street. She smelled the salt infused air in the breeze. She closed her eyes and just sat in silence, feeling her loneliness and feeling okay with it. She thought about what events led her to this place. How one small decision resulted in some dominoes falling into place, some falling out of place, and some remaining upright. She thought about where she wanted to be in a year. She thought about how little she enjoyed her work and how much time was spent there.

When she was a young girl, all she wanted was to be happy. She pictured her life like a storybook. Blue skies, a house with a white picket fence, a garden, two kids, one dog, a handsome husband, and a job that gave her fulfillment. The job piece was never clear in her mind. She had no idea what she was doing in her dream, she only knew that it brought her joy, peace, and fulfillment. It made her heart smile. She imagined herself kneeling in the garden, retrieving beautiful round vegetables. She was wearing a straw hat, pristine, fitted gloves, and jean overalls. Her two children were playing in the yard with the dog and laughing gleefully as the dog ran over with the ball. Her children were never clear either, but she knew one was a boy and one was a girl. When she entered the home to cook dinner with fresh vegetables, her husband was setting the table and lighting candles within the centerpiece on the table.

Joanie shook her head as she looked around her reality. She lived alone in a dingy apartment. There was no man in her life and there hadn't been one for years. She practically lived at the office and ate breakfast, lunch, and dinner behind her desk nine days out of ten. Her free time was spent sitting in a car crawling everywhere she needed to be, or sitting in a jam-packed train trying not to breathe because people were either sneezing, coughing, or smelled putrid. There were no children, no real relationship with her family, no friends, and no husband. She smiled sadly to herself as she realized that her life was nothing how she dreamed it would be. There was so much lost potential.

"Knock knock!" Carly called out as she walked toward the patio. Joanie squinted up at her and smiled. "Can I sit down?"

Joanie gestured to the chair next to her and Carly plopped down. "I didn't realize you were back! I brought you some leftover breakfast from this morning if you are hungry." She handed Joanie a plate filled with pancakes, a side of syrup, and a bowl of fresh fruit.

Joanie took the food and started eating the strawberries with her fingers. "Thanks! I am starving!," Joanie flashed her a genuine smile. "Sorry I didn't pop in yesterday. I have a lot on my mind," she said sadly.

Carly leaned forward and placed her chin in her cupped hands. "Yeah, about that..." she started and stopped. "I saw the articles this morning. Is it true that the Tribune is being sold?" Joanie pursed her lips and nodded slowly. "What does that mean?" Carly asked. "I mean, what does that mean for you?"

Joanie shrugged her shoulders. She honestly didn't know. "I don't know. I won't know until August 15th. The good thing is that I am kind of in a management position so I would hope they would find value in my skills, but there is no guarantee they want me and there is no guarantee that I will want them.

# An Unfinished Story

I have been there forever. I haven't been on a job interview in over 15 years. I am almost forty, Carly. I am too old to be job hunting. I never thought I would be in this position." She felt tears build up behind her eyes and refused to let the warm, salty liquid spill onto her cheeks.

Carly leaned across her chair and gave Joanie an awkward hug. Joanie remained sitting against the chair back and leaned her body toward Carly without moving her arms. "I read your article that you wrote about The Willowside." Carly said. "That was beautiful!"

Joanie smiled, "You're welcome. Thank you for being a great interviewee. It absolutely made my job that much easier."

After a few moments of silence, Carly said, "You know, you are welcome to stay here as long as you want. I like having you around."

Joanie didn't know what she wanted. She was just sitting and thinking about how many failures occurred in her life and how her dreams were never fulfilled. They were never even attempted to be fulfilled. "I thought I would be there forever. Not because I love it, but because it is comfortable. I know my job, I know the people, and I know how to manage people. The idea of applying for a new job or a new career is terrifying. What if I apply for something and I don't get it? What if I do get it and then I realize that I hate it? Do you think security is more important than passion?" Joanie leaned forward and searched Carly's eyes for guidance.

"Well, what is your passion?" Carly asked.

"I don't know! I don't know if I have any passions! What if I am a passionless person who is never going to find happiness?" Joanie leaned into her hands and wiped the tears away. They weren't tears of sadness but were tears of frustration and despair.

"Well..." Carly began. "I don't know you very well, so I certainly hope I am not overstepping, but from one girl to the next, I think you deserve to be happy. And if that means you leave your job and try something totally out of character but brings you joy, I think you need to do it. What is worse than taking risks and failing is not taking risks and wondering for the rest of your life where your life would be if you were just brave enough to follow your heart."

Joanie nodded as she swallowed back her tears. She felt so lost and so overwhelmed. She closed her eyes and let her senses calm her mind. A few minutes later, Joanie opened one eye and saw that Carly was still sitting next to her with her head back taking in the warmth of the rays of sunshine.

Later that day, Joanie reached out to Joe and asked if he would be available to meet her near the police station. There was a small park next to the police station overlooking the ocean. She was hoping Joe would be willing to give her a tour of where he worked so she could explain the intricacies of working on a small police force. She was curious what the atmosphere felt like. She wondered if people would be buzzing around, if phones would be ringing, or if there would be a steady flow of foot traffic as people entered and exited the doors.

They agreed on meeting the next day right around lunch. Before leaving the carriage house, Joanie looked at herself in the mirror. Her hair was frizzy with the humidity so she pulled it back into a low ponytail. She wet her hands under the bathroom faucet and smoothed back the flyaways around her face. She decided on a yellow sundress and thought it was too dressy. She changed into her favorite pair of jeans and a form fitting white t-shirt. She threw on a pair of bright red, wooden beads to give her bland outfit a pop of color. She put in silver hoops and grabbed the only lip gloss in her bag. It definitely wasn't much, but she felt comfortable and confident. She ignored the nerves in her belly, grabbed her purse, and headed out the door.

Joanie was the first to arrive at the park and sat down on a wooden bench facing the surf. There were a few swimmers who braved the cool water. There was a little girl walking with a woman along the water collecting what appeared to be seashells in a yellow plastic bucket. There was a man

## An Unfinished Story

throwing a frisbee to a golden retriever. Even though it wasn't hot, there was still activity on the beach. Joanie loved watching people when they least expected it. She felt that the beauty of small, mundane tasks shone through because there were no expectations of the task and people could just be as they were.

Across the grass, Joanie saw Joe. Her stomach alerted her to her new brain before her brain processed what her eyes saw. She looked down at her feet, not really understanding what her body was telling her. She looked across the field and saw his tall, lean body walking toward her. He was wearing blue jeans that were tight, but not too tight. He had on a baseball hat, which shielded his eyes. She hoped he didn't realize she was watching him. The idea of him watching her without her knowing made her stomach dance even more. She put on a big grin and walked toward him.

"Hi!" she called out. "Thank you for meeting with me!" He smiled at her with his white, straight teeth, and full lips. "I, uh..." Joanie stammered. She didn't like talking to people in general, and now she had to talk to someone that she clearly found extremely attractive. "I, uh, was hoping I could ask you some more questions about work. I have to have another article by Thursday morning. I was hoping you could give me a tour of the station?"

"Ah, I see. So you are just using me to get ahead at work, eh?" Joe smiled as he sat down on the bench. "And what do I get for helping you out, yet again?" She couldn't help but hear the flirtation behind his words.

"Well...what would you like?" She bowed her head down and looked up at him through her lashes. Joanie couldn't believe she was flirting back. It was like every movie she ever saw was taking over her body. Her mind was screaming, *What are you doing?* but her actions were in control. She couldn't stop the coyness even if she tried.

"Dinner. Tonight. And then, anything you need, I will say yes." Joe looked deeply into her eyes. He held her gaze like it was magic. She tried to break away but struggled and found herself fumbling with the keychain in her hand.

"First you show me what I want and then you get what you want," Joanie watched his hair gently move in the breeze. His thick, dark hair was taunting and daring her fingers to comb through it. She wanted to feel his head, touch his hair, and kiss his forehead. She quickly shook her head. What was she doing? She was working. She could not get caught up in a remarkably attractive man who may or may not have a girlfriend. She made a note to talk to Carly when she got back. "Are you ready to give me a tour?" Joanie jumped up from the bench, threw her bag over her shoulder, and started walking toward the police station

# Chapter 9

When Joanie got back to the carriage house, she saw Carly watering the garden bed directly in front of The Willowside main house. "Hey Carly!" Joanie called out. She didn't want to startle her. Carly turned and gave Joanie a wave. "Hey, can I talk to you about something?" she sheepishly asked.

"Sure, what's up?" Carly responded.

"I wanted to talk to you about your cousin, Joe. What is his story?" Joanie didn't have time for small talk. She had to work on her article and get ready for dinner.

Carly furrowed her eyebrows. "What do you mean?"

"I mean," Joanie began, "is he dating anyone? Has he had a lot of girlfriends before? Does he have any kids?"

Carly laughed. "No, Joanie, he doesn't have a girlfriend and he certainly doesn't have any kids. Well, none that I am aware of at least. If he has a girlfriend or kids, they certainly do not live here. He left Block Island after high school and came back a few years later. Ever since he came back, he has been single. It's not like there are a lot of dating options on the island and if he did have a girlfriend at one time or another, it would have absolutely gotten back to me. This place is small and news travels fast. I think he has just been working a lot and spending time at his parent's farm."

"Oh, did he take over the farm?" Joanie asked.

"Yes. Kind of. They left it to him when they died. The mortgage was paid off so all he had to do was pay taxes. I don't think he wanted to move back, but free rent is free rent and he really didn't have any reason not to. I know the farm

## An Unfinished Story

isn't producing anything but the land sure is pretty. Why do you ask?" Carly questioned.

"He asked me out to dinner. Tonight. I wanted to say no because I am here working, but the word yes came out of my mouth. I just wanted to make sure he wasn't a serial killer or the father of three," the words tumbled out of Joanie's mouth. "And I have nothing to wear because I didn't pack anything dinner worthy. Would you mind helping me?" she pleaded.

Carly smiled and nodded her head. The girls entered Carly's apartment and went to work.
*********************************************************************
**********************************

Carly sat at the kitchen table in her apartment and opened her computer. She had emails from the booking websites and it seemed that her guest rooms were completely booked until Labor Day. That was usually when things started to slow down. Kids went back to school, the weather started to get cooler, and the ferries travelled less frequently. Even though things slowed down, Carly still couldn't get away beyond her weekly trip to the mainland to care for her mother. Carly tried not to feel resentful toward every other woman out there, but it was hard when you felt trapped in a life you didn't choose.

Carly thought about fall and what exactly it foreshadowed. No new faces, darkened shops and quiet nights would soon characterize her days. Winter could be tough on the island because although they didn't get a lot of snow, they did get a lot of ice, rain, and wind. Carly knew that when power was lost because of a storm during the quiet season, it could be weeks before things were fully restored. That made it especially hard for her because she had to rely on cellular towers to manage the incoming appointments and reservations at The Willowside.

Carly pulled out her calendar and wrote down the new reservations. Even though she had no control of how busy the house was, it helped her plan her week to see how much prep time she needed to get the bedrooms ready for the newest visitors. It was important that their first impression of her was perfect and the bedrooms were clean and pristine. Anything less than a 4-star rating on Tripadvisor or Yelp could destroy her livelihood.

    Carly wished that she could magically beam herself to the coast of Maine. Often when she went to sleep at night she fell asleep to images of her past. When she was younger, she was full of love and full of life. She wouldn't think twice about dancing in the rain, going to the beach and searching for the perfect shell, dancing all night long at the cafe in town, or ordering a 10 lb lobster just because she could.

    Living with a fisherman was hard because the money was inconsistent but the fun they had was irreplaceable. They had lived in a studio apartment in the city of Portland and often lived on rice and beans or whatever food was accidentally made at the restaurant. John used to joke that he should call the restaurant, order some food, and never pick it up so they could eat the leftover food at home, but they never did. Usually the food she got to bring home was because the customer ordered a dish without mushrooms and the cook wasn't paying attention or the waitress wasn't clear in the order. It wasn't an easy time in her life, but she was young and in love and didn't care.

    As Carly reflected on her life, she realized that those years were the most rewarding because her future wasn't mapped out for her. She could go wherever she wanted and do whatever she wanted whenever she wanted. During the summer, John was never home because it was prime lobster season, so Carly tried to pick up double shifts to compensate for the slowness in winter. Winter was tough because John was out of work, but they managed with the money squirrelled away from the summer before and the contentment they shared just being together.

    Carly closed her computer and looked at her calendar again. It didn't look like there would ever be a time when she could get away again. She had an urge to run away and never look back. She wanted to go back to Maine where she didn't

## An Unfinished Story

know anyone and no one cared if she stayed home, went out, or ran through the streets in celebration of her birthday. Suddenly the walls in the kitchen were slowly closing in on her.

She didn't know what had gotten into her. It could have been the fact that Joanie was on a date, it could have been because she would be celebrating her 40th birthday soon, or it could have been because her life was nothing like what she planned, but she reached for her computer again and double clicked on the PeoplePlace icon. Carly pulled up the search bar and typed John Nichols. Apparently there were eight John Nichols in the world (or at least on PeoplePlace), but Carly recognized her John Nichols immediately. She quickly clicked on his profile and scanned his wall. She saw pictures of him holding a fish, sitting on a boat, sitting outside around a firepit, and drinking a beer. None of the pictures gave Carly a clue as to what his relationship status was. She didn't want to contact him if he was married or had children, but she didn't see any sign on PeoplePlace saying yes.

Before she could stop herself, she clicked add friend. Then she clicked on messenger and typed: *Hi John. It's me, Carly. I was thinking of you tonight and hope that you are doing well.* She stopped. Was that it? There was so much she wanted to say but was afraid to open up and be vulnerable. She decided to wait until he responded before revealing too much of herself and hit the Enter key. That was that. The damage was done. Either he would respond or he would not respond, and either way Carly would be okay with it. She closed her laptop again, grabbed a beer, and watched When Harry Met Sally, which was one of the movies she saw with John. She crossed her fingers that he would respond.

*********************************************************************
*****************************

Joanie dropped herself onto the bed and stared at the ceiling. She was wearing a pair of tight black pants that were fitted to the ankle with black strappy sandals and a white blouse with a black camisole underneath. The light from her nightstand was emitting a beige hue and causing shadows to dance on her ceiling as the cars drove by. She stayed like that for what felt like hours. She faintly listened to the radio that was still playing in the kitchen that she forgot to turn off before she left for dinner. Delilah's voice soothed a listener who was missing her deployed husband. Joanie couldn't really focus but her heart went out to the woman.

    She sat up in bed and looked at her hands. At the end of the evening, Joe graciously grabbed her hand as they exited the restaurant. He told her he had a great evening and wanted to get together again. He looked handsome in his dark blue jeans that looked like they had been recently washed and green polo shirt. The green of the shirt matched his eyes. He was cleanly shaven, which was a look Joanie loved. Just seeing him as she walked toward him on the sidewalk was enough to get her belly flipping and her heart racing.

    Conversation during dinner was easier than she expected, especially with her nerves running in every direction. He took her out to a cute Italian restaurant that had small bistro tables, candles, and white tablecloths. Joanie laughed that this type of place was a terrible choice because more food ended up on her clothes than in her mouth, but Joe returned the smile and said he was a slob from all those years living alone and eating in the recliner in front of his television. In a different time, Joanie would have found that information to be a turn off but tonight she found it endearing.

    They talked about a variety of topics, mostly introduced by Joe. Joanie always wondered just how much personal information was adequate to give on a first date. She didn't know anything about him and wanted to know everything, but didn't know how to ask without coming off as nosey or desperate. Joe led the conversation the entire night but Joanie counter questioned everything he asked. She learned that he wanted to be a police officer ever since he was a little boy and always imagined himself in a big city where crime was common and the police station was busy. He enjoyed

## An Unfinished Story

working in Providence but it was lonely even though he was always surrounded by people.

He was also broke during that time of his life. He was working fifty hours a week, living in a closet-sized apartment in a bad neighborhood, and was struggling with his girlfriend. He worked so much, all he wanted to do on his time off was sleep and she didn't understand that. She always took it personal and blamed their issues on his work schedule.

Joe's girlfriend, Sasha, was younger than he was and wanted a boyfriend who would be there every time she called. Joe couldn't do that because his work schedule was crazy. She wanted a boyfriend who would spoil her with the latest Tiffany necklace or surprise her with a fancy dinner and a broadway show. Joe couldn't do that either because he was barely making enough money to afford an apartment with both a separate living room and bedroom. He felt completely inadequate around her and it was clear that she felt like he wasn't good enough for her.

Their relationship quickly fizzled out and Joe's rent was due. He was renting month to month and decided to pack up and move home. He would still be able to apply for jobs, it would just make it harder for him to get a position with a gap in his work history. His parents welcomed him with wide, open arms because they were saddened the day he left and always knew he would be back.

His parents took a trip to Florida to celebrate their wedding anniversary and decided to drive because his mother was fearful of flying. She had only flown once before and then 9/11 happened and she decided she would never fly again. She didn't want to put her life in the hands of a complete stranger. So they rented a car and drove to Florida over three days.

During this time, Joe had applied for a position on Block Island because rumor had it that Officer O'Connell was getting married to a woman from New York who had no desire to move to a tiny island. While Joe was waiting for Officer O'Connell to put in his resignation, he worked with Lucas and

Logan at the fish market. It was a great opportunity to network with locals and tourists alike.

While his parents were driving home from their beachside vacation, a tractor trailer swerved into the right light from the middle lane and smashed into his parents small SUV. According to the police report, the driver fell asleep and his parents were in the wrong place at the wrong time. There was nothing his dad could have done to avoid the collision and that was it. They were gone.

"That was the story of why I left and why I came back." Joe took a sip of beer and waited for Joanie to respond.

Joanie was surprised at how much information about his past he divulged, but was thankful that he felt comfortable enough around her to tell her to tell her so much about his past.

After the waitress delivered their meals, Joe requested, "Tell me your story."

Joanie felt uncomfortable talking about herself because it seemed so mundane compared to what he had experienced. "Well, let's see," she started slowly. "I often wonder what my life would be like if I was born into another family. My life has been predictable. I have two parents, one sister, and have been working at the same company for the last fifteen years. My family isn't really close, I don't even know if my sister and I would be considered friends, and I really don't have any friends to speak of, except for Carly and work colleagues. I feel like there is so much more out there for me, but I just don't know what it is or how to get there. And that is my boring life story." She giggled because the wine was starting to get to her head. She was relieved that her life story got them off the topic of his dead parents. Joanie noted not to bring them up again.

As the alcohol started to flow through her veins, Joanie's muscles relaxed, her words formed easier, and her laughter increased. She felt amazing and stopped worrying if she was making too much eye contact, not enough contact, laughing

## An Unfinished Story

too much, or laughing too little. By the end of the night, she was present in the moment and loving every second.

After dinner, they walked along the water and stared at the giant, bright, yellow moon. They searched for the face of the man on the moon and described the shapes of the clouds as they rolled by. Joanie saw an elephant riding a motorcycle and Joe saw three balloons. The moonlight illuminated the waves lapping against the rocks. In that moment, Joe leaned over and kissed Joanie. It was a gentle kiss that lingered longer than it should have. Joanie found herself standing on her tiptoes leaning into him because she couldn't feel him enough. She was yearning for more. Joe pulled away and offered to walk her home. Joanie tried her best to hide her disappointment and smiled up at him. On the walk home he asked if she wanted to see him again and she grabbed his hand in confirmation.

Joanie thought about their night while sitting on her bed. Her head felt foggy and her body felt hot. She touched her hand, her arm, and her lips. She slithered out of Carly's clothes and climbed into the shower. The heat from the water fogged up the mirror and made it hard to breathe. Joanie climbed into bed wearing clean pajamas and dreamt of the night she just had been dreaming about for years.

# Chapter 10

The next morning, Carly groggily opened her laptop. *Please no response. Please no response. Please no response,* she silently chanted to herself. She had been thinking the past few days about what she did and wondered if there was any way she could delete the message she sent the previous night. Her brain was on fast forward and bouncing from one idea to the next. The last time she saw John was not a pleasant experience. She called him selfish for choosing Maine instead of her. She cried. She begged him to stay. She sat in her car and screamed at the top of her lungs, banging her hands against the dashboard. She felt like she had wasted time on a man who wasn't willing to waste his time on her. She deleted his phone number from her phone and unfriended him on PeoplePlace. When he said he wasn't willing to stay with her, she decided she was not willing to keep trying and the relationship quickly ended. It ended cold turkey and Carly got wrapped up in the details of running a bed and breakfast and managing her mother's health. She had so much to think about at her new life and old home, she was unable to think about John. And that was where their story ended. Until now.

Carly quickly opened PeoplePlace to find nine new notifications from the night before and one message. *Crap.* Carly closed her eyes as she clicked on the message. She slowly opened one eye to see who the message was from. It was from him. Carly quickly opened both eyes and read the message in his voice. *Hi Carly. I haven't heard from you in awhile. How is Block Island? Things up in Maine are going*

# An Unfinished Story

*well. It's been a busy season so far. Do you need anything or were you just truly just saying hi?* He closed out the conversation with a smiley face emoji, possibly to lighten the mood. She quickly checked her notifications and found that he accepted her friend request.

Carly scanned his profile looking for clues about his life. From what she could see, there was no girlfriend in the picture. She closed her laptop and sighed deeply. Life didn't stop, so she grabbed her mother's laundry and headed toward the ferry to ride back to the mainland. She decided to write back once she had a few hours to figure out what she wanted to say.

The weather was overcast and the ferry was emptier than usual. She sat on the deck and felt the cool air and ocean mist blow across her face. Today she was dreading this visit because she didn't get a lot of sleep the night before and these visits were always so draining. Carly closed her eyes and pretended she was on a beach in Aruba. She imagined the blue green water, the colorful coral reef, and the warm sun. She imagined the fruity drinks with little umbrellas, the colorful beach umbrellas protecting her skin, and the tan bodies on the beach. When she opened her eyes, she was facing the streets of New London, awaiting her trek to the nursing home.

When she got to the room, she found Ruth sleeping and a nurse checking her vitals. "Hi Martha," Carly said upon entering. Martha turned her head over her shoulder and made eye contact as she silently counted to herself. Carly dropped her bag on the pink chair next to the window.

"Hi Carly," Martha said as she picked up her chart.

"How is she doing?" Carly asked nodding toward the bed. "Usually she isn't napping until after lunch."

"Your mom has been battling a temperature all night. She slept through breakfast and was agitated during the night when we tried to give her her medication. She probably is exhausted from fighting us." Martha reported.

"What do you think it is?" Carly worriedly asked.

## Erica Haraldsen

"We don't know if it is just a virus or something more. We have been tracking her food intake at meals and she seems to be coughing more frequently. We have her scheduled for an X-Ray to rule out pneumonia later today. Hopefully it is just a virus."

Carly thought about the ferry that she traveled on every week and wondered if she brought in germs from the handrails or seats. No one called her with their concern, so Carly decided if they weren't overly worried, she wouldn't be overly worried either. She made a mental note to grab hand sanitizer and keep it in her bag so she could sanitize her hands whenever she got off the boat.

That afternoon Carly sat in the pink chair overlooking the green field, waiting for her mother to wake up. Every now and then her eyes opened and she asked to be repositioned or asked for water, but most of the visit was spent in silence.

Carly looked at the black and white photos framed on her dresser. There was a photo of her mother and father on their wedding day holding hands on the dance floor. There was curiosity, delight, and laughter in their eyes. There was a second photo of her mother, father, and herself when she was a little girl. Carly was about eight years old and was squeezed between both of her parents on their loveseat wearing their Sunday best. A christmas tree was behind the loveseat covered in lights, garland, and tinsel. When her parents did Christmas, they went all out with the decorations! *By today's standards, this tree would be gaudy,* Carly thought, *but look how happy we were!* The family of three had Christmas bows on their heads and tinsel in their hair. They were all laughing with wide mouths and squinty eyes. Carly knew that her family was the most important thing her mother had.

Her mother looked so weak and frail. Carly never noticed before, but it seemed like she lost weight. The neckline of her floral nightgown hung loosely around her bony shoulders. Her facial bones were more pronounced than Carly recalled, and her hair was a complete disaster against her pillow.

## An Unfinished Story

When they were eating, Ruth asked Carly about The Willowside and the ferry ride over. Carly was pleased that although her body was fighting, her mind seemed okay. She didn't want to leave her mother at the end of the day and worried that something terrible would happen. The nurse promised her that the x-ray would be done by 5 pm and they would call with the results.

Carly reluctantly left because she had to get back to prep the inn for the next round of guests. After she returned home, she called the nursing home to check in on her mother. They said that she had pneumonia and was placed on antibiotics. The speech-therapist came in at dinner to do a swallowing evaluation and Ruth was placed on a ground diet and thickened liquids. Carly knew that her mother was going to put up a fight at every meal.

According to her mother, food was for enjoyment, not for survival. She spent most of her life cooking home cooked meals for Carly's father and the guests at The Willowside. Not being able to eat her favorite foods was a huge adjustment when she first had her stroke. Ground diet and thickened liquids might just kill her. Carly promised to be back next week and requested they call if anything came up. She hung up the phone and slumped into the couch thinking about just how short life was.

She looked around her living quarters. The 450 square foot "apartment" still had pieces of her parents scattered throughout the rooms. The old teapot that her grandmother and mother used to drink from was still sitting on the counter. Carly didn't drink tea, yet the memory of her grandmother was strong when she looked at the teapot and she couldn't bear to get rid of it. The mantle was adorned with Hummels that her parents collected over the years. The green armchair that her dad would sit in every night to watch baseball was still placed directly in front of the television. Carly found these relics comforting. They had become part of her because they were part of her history.

Erica Haraldsen

When her mom went into the nursing home, this apartment was a mess. It was cluttered with old newspapers and magazines that her dad would read and save. There were individual jars of spices, from who knows what year, lining the kitchen cabinets. The closets were overflowing with clothes, bedsheets, blankets, and towels that were worn, tattered, and smelled like mildew. After Carly's father passed away, her mother ran out of time during the day and couldn't quite keep the apartment up to her typical standards. Carly spent the first month throwing out trash and nicknacks that her mother would never see again. It was an expensive endeavor because anything on the island was expensive, but Carly felt much better when the memories of her parents were minimized.

She hated feeling trapped. She was a grown, independent woman, and she still felt like a 10 year old girl trapped under her parents rules. Usually these feelings emerged when she thought about her life in Maine, and lately she had been thinking about Maine a lot. Sometimes she wondered what would have happened had she never returned back to the island. She wondered if she would be better off or if she would be married, have kids, or what her job would be. It made her sad that she blew so much potential for her future. What exactly was she holding onto The Willowside for? At first she thought that the move would be temporary just until her mother got back on her feet, but it's been years now. She wasn't coming back.

Carly looked down at her calendar. Three more people were checking in on Friday and two guest rooms were still occupied. She made her grocery list for the weekend, folded the linens, restocked the brochures and activity center, and paid some bills. Carly sighed. Just another day in the life of an innkeeper.

\*\*\*\*\*\*\*\*\*\*\*\*\*\*\*\*\*\*\*\*\*\*\*\*\*\*\*\*\*\*\*\*\*\*\*\*\*\*\*\*\*\*\*\*\*\*\*\*\*\*\*\*\*\*\*\*\*\*\*\*\*\*\*\*\*\*\*\*
\*\*\*\*\*\*\*\*\*\*\*\*\*\*\*\*\*\*\*\*\*\*\*\*\*\*\*\*\*\*\*\*\*\*

Joanie felt a pit slowly form in her stomach. She was nervous to come into the office. It had been about 5 days since she was last thrown into the chaos of her future. Her phone and email had been buzzing nonstop and Joanie tried to return messages, but it eventually became overwhelming so she just stopped. Her voicemail was full and her email had an automated message saying she was out of the office. Her cell phone service was spotty on the island so it wasn't a complete lie.

Joanie took a deep breath, opened the door to the office, and slowly walked in. The lights were sporadically on, which created a dim atmosphere. The sunlight was shining through the window and generated most of the light in the room. It was eerily quiet. There was no chatter, no clicking of keys on the computer, no faint music playing in the background.

"Hey Marley," Joanie called. "Is Mark here?" Marley nodded her head toward his

office. The door was closed and the lights were off. It certainly didn't look like he was there. Joanie gently knocked on the door and waited. No response. She knocked harder and waited. "Come in!" Mark's voice greeted her.

Joanie found him sitting behind his desk in a t-shirt and blue jeans. His hair was disheveled, his beard was sporadically growing in, and his eyes were darkened underneath. His laptop screen was open and papers were strewn all over the desk and floor.

"What are you doing?" Joanie asked, eyeing all the paper on the floor.

A loud, bellowing laugh erupted from Mark like a volcano spewing lava. "Well,

believe it or not, I am applying for a new job. Have you noticed that the entire office is empty? Yeah, it's been like that all week. Everyone decided that now is a great time to take all their built up vacation days. Which means no one is here. And if no one is here, there are no articles getting written. And if there are no articles, there is no paper. And if there is no paper, there is no job." Mark was speaking rapidly, cracking his knuckles above his keyboard. "So," he continued, "I am looking for another job. I have no idea what kind of job, but something. Because after this weekend when we have NOTHING," he yelled, "we ALL won't have a job!"

Joanie sat down in the chair opposite him. Her mind was racing and the sound of her blood pumping in her ears was overpowering her thoughts. No articles. No paper. No job. No articles. No paper. No job. She grabbed her cell phone and texted everyone in her department: EMERGENCY MEETING. TODAY. 3 PM AT THE OFFICE. She hit send, ran out of Mark's office to her desk, and started writing every question she had for her staff. If her job was going down, she needed to know everyone's intentions and thoughts about the buy-out.

The clock slowly ticked on. It was amazing how slowly time could pass when you were anticipating a defining moment in your life. This was it. Her make or break moment when she would either continue on the same path or bust free from her life, like a prison break. She could hear the clock ticking, hear her pen clicking non-stop, feel her knee banging against the underside of her desk like a metronome. She wasn't sure if anyone would show, but if they didn't, it was game over.

The green light on her radio sitting on the filing cabinet illuminated 12:56 pm. Joanie left the office to get some air. Even though the office was air conditioned, she felt stifled. She could feel her heart rate increasing, her palms getting sweaty, and her mind jumping around. Joanie stepped outside to the blast of car engines, horns, birds, shuffling feet, and constant chatter. She found the nearest tree and slid down the trunk. She closed her eyes, breathed in, and counted to ten.

She pulled out her cell phone and searched for jobs within all the major, yet local networks. Even if she took a paycut, she would apply. Some money was better than no money, she decided. She found a listing for a team leader for one of the local papers, which might be a nice, easy transition. She found a listing for an intern, which definitely would not work. There wasn't much out there right now. The internet was slowly killing her income potential.

# An Unfinished Story

What was she thinking, going into business for college? She decided to broaden her search, since business could really be anything? She looked for customer service positions, which were plentiful. She didn't really want to be answering calls of unhappy customers, but a job was a job and she didn't exactly have time to be picky. She saw that many of the hotels were hiring, and some of which were for manager positions. She had no experience, but was confident she could learn quickly, and discounted hotel rooms would be an added perk.

She refused to look into restaurants. Waitressing was all about communicating with people, but she couldn't quite succumb to dealing with grouchy, demanding, entitled millennials that wanted their food vegan, gluten-free, paleo, or keto only. Everyone had limitations, and Joanie knew hers fell along the line of restaurant management.

She looked at her watch. 1:38. She quickly got up from the tree and picked up a quick lunch. If she was going to confront her team, she needed to make sure her blood sugar was up. The worst thing was to have a stressful conversation when all you wanted was a chocolate bar. By the time she got back to the office, it was after 2. Joanie said a prayer that people would come.

After 40 minutes of pacing, eating chocolate, drinking coffee, checking her email, and working on her resume, Mikayla walked into the room. She was wearing baggy jeans, sneakers, a wrinkled top, and her hair was pulled back in a ponytail. It was obvious that she had no intention of working today. She sat in the chair opposite Joanie and stated, "I'm here. Where is this meeting?"

"Conference room. I will be in in one minute," she gestured toward the door. Mikayla gathered her purse and left while Joanie grabbed a pen and a notebook. She followed Mikayla into the room and sat down at the head of the table. She was waiting for four other team members and told Mikayla they would wait until 3:15 before dismissing the meeting if no one showed.

Erica Haraldsen

At 3:13, Joanie was surrounded by Mikayla and two of her five team members. She considered it a good amount since the meeting was called three hours ago and it seemed like every one of them had not been working. Mark didn't know that she was meeting with everyone and she wanted to keep it that way. He left at lunch and never returned, so Joanie thought it was a good time. She knew that if Mark was in the office, no one would voice their honest thoughts. She thought that if the office was empty, they would be more willing to tell her straight what their intentions were.

"Hi everyone!" Joanie smiled her most convincing smile that today was a regular day like any other. "I wanted to talk to you about the Lifestyle section of the paper. Does everyone have their topic for Sunday's printing?" She looked at them expectantly. Mikayla analyzed the cuticles on her already chipping fingernails. Danny flipped through the notebook he brought to the meeting. Susanna checked her phone, possibly for messages or email. Joanie wasn't sure. Joanie felt her chest tighten and her throat close. She wanted to speak but nothing was happening.

She knew that if she waited long enough, the air in the room would become so uncomfortable, someone would burst open and answer her question. So she waited. She sat down in her chair and leaned forward pressing her chin into her closed fist. She breathed in for four seconds, held it for 6 seconds, and exhaled for 8 seconds. She looked at her three officemates anxiously.

The level of noncommitment within the atmosphere was slowly drowning Joanie. She held on for as long as she could, but when she felt on the edge of a panic attack setting in, she did something she never wanted to do. She hated when her professors did it, but suddenly understood why they called people out by name. "Susanna? Are you prepared for Sunday's paper?" Susanna snapped her head up and hid her fingers in her lap.

"Actually....yes and no," Susanna spoke slowly and deliberately. Joanie knew that if she admitted to not being prepared she could be fired, and if she was fired without a new job in place, she could be in a financial mess. "I have a first draft written on that new restaurant that opened but I am waiting to interview the owner." Joanie slowly nodded. The article will be there, but the quality might be elementary, Joanie thought to herself.

"Let's try this a different way," Joanie started. She decided a different approach might get her the information. "Mark is not here, you guys. It's just us. Let me ask you, do you see yourself working here in five years?" Mikayla remained stone faced and the other two shook their heads, unsure of how to respond. "We have a lot of changes coming up. A lot of unknown, which can be really scary. I get it, you guys, I do. I am right there with you, not knowing what is going to happen. How many of you expect to be here in one year?" Again, no hands went up. That was the answer Joanie was looking for. Her ship was sinking.

"Where is Mark?" Mikayla asked. Joanie shrugged her shoulders.

"This might sound strange coming from me," Joanie started, "but if any of you need a letter of recommendation, I will gladly write it. But in the meantime, you still have a job here and you are still getting a paycheck from us. Please put forth your best effort until the future of the paper gets straightened out. That's it. Please send me your articles by Friday night. I will see you tomorrow." Joanie gathered her notebook and pen and was the first to leave the conference room and office. She needed air. She needed to think and figure out a solution quickly.

Joanie went to her apartment. It was hot and stuffy. She forgot to turn on the air conditioner before she rushed out the door for work. Joanie dropped her bag next to the door, kicked off her shoes, and turned on the air. She knelt down on the floor and leaned her face into the vents of the air conditioner. The loud, forceful breeze calmed her mind.

Joanie sat at the table and pulled out her laptop. She reviewed the article she wrote about Joe and what life was like being a policeman on Block Island. She started her article describing the police station and finished it with a personal story Joe told her about why he moved back. Joanie made a few edits and then saved. She checked her email for the other articles and of course nothing was sent. She checked her phone for text messages regarding work and she had one email from Susanna asking her for a letter of recommendation. Joanie knew she had to write it because she said she would, but she was not excited to encourage another company to take her employee.

    Joanie texted Susanna agreeing to the letter and did not ask any other questions. She then sent a group text to her staff reviewing that she needed all articles by Friday night. There was nothing else she could do, and she was heading back to Block Island tomorrow, so Joanie quickly wrote a letter of recommendation stating that Susanna was enthusiastic, driven, a great problem solver, personable, and worked well under pressure. It may not have been the best letter of recommendation ever written, but it got the job done. Joanie proofread the letter for grammatical errors and sent it to Susanna. She would have a hard copy available next week.

    Every transition back to town meant unpacking, laundry, and repacking. Joanie continued on with her day, hoping that nothing else would come up. She was looking forward to going back to Block Island. Next she was interviewing Lucas and Logan, the fishermen. She wrote down a list of questions to ask, cooked dinner, and headed to bed with a reality TV program to help her escape from her life. She couldn't wait to get off that ferry and step foot on the beautiful, pristine island, where worries seemed small and beauty was abundant.

# Chapter 11

Carly tended to the garden and hummed along to "I Love Rock N Roll" as she pulled weeds and watered. The song was playing on the radio as she opened up PeoplePlace and found another message from John. The song played in her head like an anthem. Her fingers moved to the beat of the song as she dug, pruned, and pulled.

She wrote back to John another message that didn't give away too much information. She wasn't willing to show him her heart for fear of rejection again. She told him about the inn, the weather, and a brief overview of the last five years. Every time her phone dinged she expectedly looked down hoping it was him. Sometimes it was, and sometimes it wasn't, but today they had been writing back and forth like pen pals.

He told her that he thought of her often and only wanted her to be happy. He alluded to possibly seeing her when the summer season ended and they both had free time. Carly knew that his statement was a polite gesture without any likelihood of actually occurring. She agreed and said it would be nice because that was the polite thing to say. She wasn't going to allow her heart to believe it could or would happen. By the time summer was over, there may not be any more correspondence because that was how life happened for Carly. When things were good, the bad was always right around the corner waiting to jump.

Regardless of what happened down the road, Carly was thrilled that he wrote back, that he thought of her at all, and that she was still present in his life, no matter how miniscule

## An Unfinished Story

that presence was. She continued to hum, sing, and pull until the flower bed looked clean, precise, and professional. All the while she was dreaming, not about the life she left, but about the life she was yet to have.

Her birthday was in October, which was perfect because Block Island emptied out by then. Labor Day was the last busy weekend of the season and September and October were used to take care of all the housekeeping from the summer business. Carly was not strong in math, money, or finances, so it took her twice as long to figure out if and by how much she made a profit. Her parents never ran into a problem managing their money. Carly never remembered a time when money was tight, even during the Christmas season. Her father invested in the Stock Market but did so responsibly. If Carly invested, she would be viewed as reckless and maybe even blamed if the business went under and she had to file bankruptcy.

To get through the winter months, Carly kept The Willowside open, but it was never consistent. If she did have a guest, it was usually for two nights or less, which meant that Carly was still trapped cooking, doing laundry, and being present in the house. She truly never got a break and never got to leave.

When she got back inside, she checked her phone and found one missed call and voice message. The number had a Connecticut area code and Carly immediately thought of her mother. *It had only been 48 hours, nothing could have gone wrong, could it?* She thought. The voicemail was Ruth's nursing supervisor, Sharon. *"Hi Carly, this is Sharon calling. Your mother was admitted to the hospital early this morning. She still had a fever, despite the antibiotics, her blood pressure dropped, and she was having difficulty breathing. Please call at your earliest opportunity."* The message clicked off. Carly stared at the phone, not quite sure if this was real or a joke.

She sat on the stool under the island and stared at the phone. She listened to the message again. Yes, Sharon said that she was in the hospital. Joanie felt the ball forming in her throat that prevented any sound from escaping. She felt tears filling behind her eyes and felt the pressure building until the tears exploded like a dam breaking. She felt very hot and stuffy. The air suddenly became thick and dense and difficult to breathe. Carly ran outside and sat on the doorstep, sucking in the cool air waiting for the dizziness to pass.

    She was afraid to call the nursing home. Afraid to look at her phone. Afraid to hear the voicemail again. She knew she had to call back, but there was still so much to be done to get ready for the guests. She had sheets to wash, shopping to do, and guests she had to greet. She didn't have time to be calling a hospital and listening to a nurse or doctor deliver too much information in a language she didn't understand.

    She did next what she always did when life got overwhelming. She pulled out her grandmother's tea kettle, her favorite mug, sugar, and a Lipton tea bag and proceeded to pour herself a cup of tea, despite the temperature steadily climbing past 80 degrees. *Dad, I don't know if you are with me or mom, but I need you,* Carly prayed. *I need you to stay with her. Hold her hand, whisper in her ear, and tell her to be strong.* Carly raised the mug and cheered to no one in sight, imagining that her grandmother was there to keep her company. Once Carly felt brave enough, she picked up her phone and hit "Call Back." She was immediately transferred to Sharon.

    "Hi, Sharon," Carly's voice squeaked out. The tone and pitch of her voice surprised her. She thought she was stronger than that. "It's Carly. I'm returning your call." She was hoping Sharon would tell her there was a mix up. It wasn't her mother, it was her roommate, and the new nurse on staff told her to call the wrong family.

    "Carly, I am so sorry to share this news with you. Last night we continued to watch her fever. She went to bed easily and surprisingly took her medication easily as well. Around midnight, her fever started to spike so we gave her Tylenol. When we got her up this morning, she was groggy and weak

## An Unfinished Story

but she was up. She barely touched her breakfast and needed full assistance to get dressed and use the bathroom. When the doctor arrived, he listened to her lungs and we called an ambulance. Her breathing had gotten more labored throughout the evening and her oxygen level was low but still at a safe level. This morning it had dropped. She was admitted to the hospital for pneumonia. What we were giving her for antibiotics was not strong enough and her body couldn't fight it. She will probably be there for the next 48 hours and then she will return back to us." Sharon's story spilled out of her mouth like a slow leaky tire. Carly listened but she just wanted the story to end.

"Is it just pneumonia or could it be something else as well?" Carly asked.

Sharon paused before responding. "Well," she started and then stopped. "They are monitoring her heart due to arrythmia. She never had an issue with an irregular heart beat, but sometimes the bacteria from pneumonia can travel to the heart and interfere with her heart's function."

Carly stood at the counter with a stooped posture. She watched the tears fall directly down from the crest of her cheek to the granite on the countertop. "Is it serious?" she whispered.

"Actually, it can be fatal. She is being monitored. If you have more questions, I suggest you come to the hospital and talk to the doctor," Sharon recommended.

Carly disconnected from the phone call, and the tears were immediately released in loud, heavy sobs. She had to see her mother, but how? She had three visitors showing up today for a fun time away from home. Carly's body felt numb and not her own. She had a job to do here. Life couldn't happen. She wasn't ready. She had no help and no opportunity to close down The Willowside for the weekend and couldn't afford to lose the income.

Her mother was almost 84 years old. She wasn't a spring chicken and her health definitely was weakening. Carly knew this time in her life would come when her mother would need her, but she didn't expect it to be now, during the busy season when she needed to be on the island. Carly lied on the couch and stared at the ceiling. Her mind was running in circles about what to do. How could she be in two places at once? She would ask Joanie, but Joanie wasn't due back until late tonight and Carly didn't have that much time. She had to go immediately.

    She called the only person she trusted and she knew her mother would approve. Joe hung around enough at The Willowside as a kid. He knew the basics. He knew that the beds needed linens, he knew how to cook pancakes, and he knew where everything was in the kitchen. She called half hoping he wouldn't pick up, but he did.

    "Joe. It's Carly," she spoke rapidly as she ran around the house stuffing random clothes into an overnight bag. "My mom is in the hospital with pneumonia and something is wrong with her heart. I have to go see her for a few days. Would you be able to stay at The Willowside for me? Please. I am begging you. I have no one else to ask."

    There was silence on the other end. Carly froze in place as her heart sank into her stomach. "Please," she repeated.

    "Carly, I can, but I have to work the overnight shift Saturday night and Sunday night," Joe said. *Crap. Crap. Crap. Think, think, think, Carly!* Carly thought to herself. *Of course. He works. He has a job!* Carly felt stupid for allowing that information to completely bypass her problem solving skills.

    "Can you please stay tonight? I really have to get to the hospital. If I have to come home tomorrow I will." She didn't have time to think right now, she just had to go.

    "Yes. I will be over in five minutes," Joe eventually responded.

    "Thank you! I will have everything written down for what you need to check in the guests. They should be here after three." Carly ran through her closet and bathroom and continued to stuff random items into her bag. She went into

## An Unfinished Story

The Willowside main kitchen with a pad of paper and started to furiously scribble down important information about check-in and meals. This was the first time she ever passed responsibility for The Willowside Inn to someone else. Carly prayed that when she got home the house would still be standing.

# Chapter 12

    The trek back to Block Island was long and dreary. The gray sky was coated in thick, dark clouds. Rain drops wanted to fall, but the clouds were hanging on tightly. It left a moist feel to the air, and as the boat buzzed through the water, the air felt chilly against Joanie's skin. She pulled the strings on her sweatshirt and tightened her hood around her face to keep the wind out. She knew she should go into the cabin, where it was warm and dry, but the abuse from the ocean waves grounded her.

    It was Friday. Deadline day. The day her future would become more clear. If her team didn't pull through for her, her job was toast. She knew that they needed their job, but she also knew they were frustrated and disenfranchised with the lack of information they received throughout the past month. Joanie looked to the sky and stared at the clouds as they slowly rolled by. She debated staying in Boston until tomorrow, but what was the point? Either they came through for her or they didn't. There was nothing she could do from there or from here, so she decided to continue back to Block Island. At least the atmosphere and people would keep her mind off her impending doom.

    By the time Joanie got off the ferry, she had been traveling for almost five hours. She didn't sleep much the night before and her eyes were heavy. All she wanted to do was crawl into her bed and take a nap. Perhaps when she woke up she would be feeling more hopeful and less anxious.

    Joanie made her bed in the carriage house before she left for Boston. The puffy pillows surrounded the head of the

## An Unfinished Story

bed and the floral bedspread was smooth and wrinkle-free. Joanie fell face first into the bed, kicked off her shoes, and curled into a ball under the top blanket. When she woke up, three hours had passed and it was practically dinner time. Joanie usually did her shopping on Friday, when she returned from Boston, but stopping at the market was the last thing she wanted to do today. She glanced outside her kitchenette window and saw a light on at The Willowside Inn. Joanie pulled on her jeans and headed over to see if Carly had any dinner to share. She wanted to share her week with her, for the sake of processing what had happened. Maybe Carly would have an idea about what to do if the team didn't send her their articles.

"Knock knock!" Joanie called out as she knocked twice on the back door. The back door entered into the large farmer's kitchen, where Carly prepared breakfast every morning. No one came so Joanie knocked again and then turned the door knob. It opened. "Knock knock!" she called again. She poured herself a glass of water, sat at the kitchen table and started to write a note explaining that she stopped by and wanted to talk, if Carly had nothing better to do.

Joanie heard a door from somewhere in the house close and humming that got increasingly louder. Joe walked in, wearing earbuds, navy blue slippers, tight fitting jeans, and an oversized sweatshirt. He was carrying a laundry basket and placed it on the kitchen table. Joanie smiled big and gave Joe a little wave. He dropped the basket on the counter, pulled out his earbuds, and said, "Heeeeeeeeeeeeeeeeey! I didn't know you were here!"

"I was hoping to grab a bite to eat with Carly. Is she here? What are you doing here? Your laundry?" she giggled at seeing him taking on the role as housewife.

Joe smiled back at her, flashing his straight, white teeth. "Actually, no, she's not here. There was a family emergency. She is back in Connecticut. Hopefully it is only until tomorrow because I have to work tomorrow night. She needed me to stay here to greet the guests and make sure they were set up and fed in the morning," Joe explained.

"Do you need any help? I could really use a distraction," Joanie admitted.

"Right now? No help. Just folding laundry. Tomorrow morning though, I could probably use help. I haven't cooked for more than just myself since.....ever. And the only breakfast food I know how to make is cereal. And toast. I was debating about getting breakfast catered for tomorrow but if you can help, that would be awesome!"

Joanie thought about it. Tomorrow morning she would wake up to hopefully four emails with four articles ready to go. If she got the articles, she would help Joe with a pep in her step due to the level of relief within her body. If the articles did not come, would she want to be in the kitchen? She probably would want to be crying in her bed, wallowing in the fact that she was jobless, poor, and possibly homeless. If she was cooking with Joe, she may not be the best company, but at least she wouldn't be thinking about her future.

"Yes!" Joanie cried, "That would be wonderful! I have to warn you though. I make some mean bacon. As we say up North," she chided, "it is wicked good!"

"Thank you!" Joe grabbed her hands in his and kissed the top of her hand. "You have officially saved my life and possibly saved the guest experience for tomorrow. Are you hungry? I ordered pizza. It should be here in about seven minutes," Joe invited Joanie to stay.

"That sounds delicious! I am starving," Joanie said. That night her and Joe had an impromptu date, although they would never call it a date, and sat in the kitchen with pepperoni pizza, a few beers, and ice cream for dessert. Joanie couldn't believe how quickly her day had changed. The entire evening with Joe, she did not worry about checking her email or messages. She didn't tell him anything about work because she didn't want to be a drag and dampen the mood. Instead she only told him the good stuff about her life. He listened intently and she felt amazing. At the end of the night she gave

## An Unfinished Story

him a kiss and said, "I will see you bright and early, sunshine," and strutted across the lawn to the carriage house. She could feel his eyes examining her body as she walked away.

The next morning, Joanie woke up with the sunrise. The birds were chirping, the coffee was brewing, and the smell of java was filling the house. Joanie fell asleep and slept hard all night. She didn't recall having any dreams, but did fall asleep thinking about Joe, their impromptu dinner, and imagining what breakfast would bring. Joanie pulled open the bureau drawers and searched for something comfortable yet sexy. She only brought what she needed because she wasn't on vacation, so her choices were slim. She had a pair of jeans that hugged her body in all the right places, a pair of black yoga pants that accentuated her curves, and a pair of shorts that her mother would deem as acceptable hiking attire. Joanie pulled out the jeans and a form fitting plaid button down with a black camisole underneath.

She looked herself over and placed her red beaded necklace over her head. Perfect. Now for hair and makeup, she thought. Joanie usually wore her hair in a ponytail because it was easiest, but felt that a ponytail might be too tom-boyish. It might send the wrong idea. Instead she pulled out her hair, drenched it under the shower head, and squeezed a dollop of mousse onto the ends. It wasn't what she imagined from Pinterest or Instagram, but it was certainly sexier than a ponytail. For makeup, all she had was lip gloss and mascara. It was only 6:15 am and the people staying at the guest house certainly weren't expecting someone to look like they were working a cocktail party. She felt confident and comfortable with herself. She walked toward the main house with a smile plastered across her face.

When she walked into the kitchen, Joe was already scurrying around like a lost little boy. Not only did he know where nothing was, but he also didn't know the first thing about cooking. "I am here to help!" Joanie announced as the door shut behind her.

"Great!" Joe said, "I have no idea where to start." He awkwardly approached her and touched her hair. "You look beautiful," he whispered. Joanie's eyes were locked into his and she couldn't break his trance. She had so much running through her head but couldn't get the words out. Instead she smiled, leaned in and gave him a hug. "Good morning!" she responded, her face getting hot as her inner voice chastised her for not returning the compliment.

"We need to make pancakes, sausage, bacon, toast, and scrambled eggs," Joe rattled off, reading the list Carly left. "What can I do and what will you do?"

Joanie pulled out the pancake mix box and threw it towards him. The box crashed into his chest and a cloud of mix puffed out the top of the box. Joanie giggled and tousled Joe's hair, shaking out the extra batter mix. She giggled and said, "I am so sorry! Here, you can mix the batter and I will prepare the eggs. Let's throw the sausage and bacon on the stove now since it takes a while." Joe took a handful of dry mix and threw it towards her playfully with a smile. It coated Joanie's face and they both laughed.

As the morning wore on, they worked in silence, listening to the radio play one hit wonder hits from the 1980s. Joanie danced around the kitchen, quietly singing to herself, and giving cooking hints to Joe. They made a good team, Joanie decided. Joanie did most of the cooking, while Joe set the tables. By the time he was done, it was 7:30 and people were coming down for breakfast. After everyone else was served, Joe and Joanie sat at the private dining table in the kitchen and ate together.

Joanie always struggled with conversation, but she felt surprisingly comfortable with Joe. It was almost like they had known each other for years. Every time Joe would look at her from the corner of his eye, her stomach would do a little flip and a turn. Her hands grew clammy and her breathing grew shallow. The feelings were too much for her to process or understand, so she clumsily got up from the table, cleared her plate, and told Joe she had to go home and get to work. He

## An Unfinished Story

watched her leave, wondering what he said or did that upset her.

*******************************************************************************************************

Ruth was laying in the hospital bed, eyes closed, quietly breathing like she was taking her usual nap. There were tubes coming out of her nose and she was hooked up to beeping monitors that played the drumbeat to Carly's favorite song. The clock tick-tocked rhythmically and her roommate had the television playing at full volume. Carly knew Judge Judy was getting annoyed at the plaintiff and she hadn't even seen the case.

Carly arrived yesterday evening and stayed at a hotel within walking distance to the hospital. Last night she met with the doctor who told her that the antibiotics were not working as quickly as they would have liked. Ruth was in a state of congestive heart failure, which complicated the matter, but they were doing everything they could to get her back to the nursing home.

Carly didn't feel relieved after leaving the hospital last night. She felt scared, worried, and anxious. She felt like her world was spinning out of control. She laid in the bed at the hotel, with it's thin, worn bedcover showing signs of cigarette burns and tears, feeling completely numb. She prayed she didn't bring home bed bugs, closed her eyes, and restlessly slept the night away.

She immediately came back to the hospital the next morning, praying that there would be a change. Carly sat in the chair directly across from her mother all morning. No words were exchanged, no greetings or smiles occurred, and Carly continued to sit. She wasn't going to leave her mother's side, she decided, until Ruth left the hospital.

Carly called The Willowside to see how the morning breakfast went. She was nervous that Joe would somehow screw it up because he had zero experience in the hospitality field, but he was her only option.

"Hello, welcome to The Willowside!" a deep voice bellowed. She could hear in his voice that he was smiling.

"Hi, Joe! It's Carly. I wanted to call and see how your twenty-four hours went."

"Carly, hi! It actually went great! Last night Joanie popped over because she needed to talk to you, and she saw that I was in way over my head, so she helped me figure out the morning and came over to help me cook," Carly could hear music in the background. "I think," he continued, "the morning was a success. No one died of food poisoning, no one choked, and one person even asked for seconds. How is your mom?" he interrupted his own thoughts with the reason why he was there in the first place.

"Well, not great. That's why I was calling. You have to go to work tonight, right? I am going to cancel all the reservations for the week. I can't leave my mom." It killed her to say that because she needed the money, but if she did go back today, she wouldn't be able to focus. It would be a disaster.

Joe was silent. "Carly, we killed it last night. Let me talk to Joanie. She is here for the next three days. Maybe her and I can figure out a schedule just to keep the doors open for a few more days. That way you don't lose as much money if you do have to cancel next week's reservations."

Carly sat for a moment. She had never given up control of the inn since she took over a few years back. She never even had an employee because winters were so hard. "I can't pay you," she said bluntly.

"Carly, we are family! Think about it. Call me before my shift, let me know, and give your mom a hug and kiss from me," Joe said confidently.

Carly hung up the phone and continued to sit, staring at her mother. She couldn't believe this is where her life took her. She knew she would deal with this eventually, but she wasn't even forty yet! Her mom should be healthy, cooking breakfast for the guests, gardening in the spring and knitting in the winter. She should not be this sick this early on in Carly's life. Carly fought back tears from sliding out the corner of her eye

## An Unfinished Story

and stared out the window. She was afraid and she wasn't going to let that fear swallow her whole.

The nurse walked in and smiled at Carly. "Just taking vitals," she said, seeing the concern across Carly's face.

"How is she?" Cary asked quickly.

The nurse took a few minutes to read numbers and document on her chart and then approached Carly. She sat down next to Carly in the chair opposite her. "Her heart rate is down, her blood pressure is low, and her respiration is slower than we would like. The doctor is here doing his rounds. He will be in shortly if you wanted to wait. He might be able to answer your questions more about where we go from here," she meekly smiled at Carly.

Carly sat for what felt like an eternity. The breakfast trays came out, the lunch trays came in, and no magical doctor appeared. Carly's brain had completely shut off. She couldn't think about her mom, couldn't think about The Willowside, and certainly couldn't think about when she would return. To pass the time waiting, she opened up PeoplePlace. There was a message notification and Carly felt her heart jump against her chest.

*Hi Carly! I was thinking of you this morning. Do you ever come back to Maine to visit? I would love to see you.*

Carly couldn't help but smile. This was her ray of sunshine during this overwise draining day. This message gave her hope that life would eventually get better. She quickly wrote back and sent it before she could proofread, edit, or change her mind.

*Hi John! No, unfortunately I haven't been back to Maine since I left. It's just too hard to leave the inn for more than a day. Hopefully soon I will be back up there, eating fresh lobster on the shores of Portland. If that day ever comes, I will certainly let you know.*

Carly waited a few moments to see if he would write back, but the message wasn't even seen, so she slipped her phone back into her bag and looked at her mom. No change. Eyes still closed. Monitors still beeping.

Carly heard a rap on the door and she quickly stood up from her chair. A man stuck out his hand and said, "Hi, I am Doctor Meyer. I have been overseeing your mother's case." Carly took his hand, introduced herself and sat back down, waiting for any news.

"Your mother is 84 years old and has cognitive weaknesses. She was admitted for pneumonia but also has congestive heart failure. When she arrived, the pneumonia was in both lungs, her blood pressure was low, and her respiration was low. Your mother is very sick. We are doing everything we can, but because of her age, her recovery is going to be twice as long as a healthy young person, like yourself. The antibiotic is working, but not nearly as quickly as we would have expected, and the reason is because she is allergic to the number one antibiotic used to treat pneumonia. She is fighting to get healthy, but I don't want to give you false hope and I don't want to scare you. Your mother is very sick and we are doing everything we can to get her healthy again." The doctor stared into her eyes, waiting for a response or a reaction, but Carly had nothing to give. She stared at her mom, lying peacefully in the bed, and the tears started to fall. The doctor slowly inched his way out of the room as if he was never there in the first place.

*********************************************************************************************************

Joanie's eyes sprung open with a start and looked at the clock. It was a little after midnight, and Joanie felt like she was forgetting something. *Shit, shit shit,* she thought. The paper. She ran to her laptop and pulled up her email. She was supposed to make sure everything was ready for the printer yesterday! Joanie was so wrapped up in helping Carly and hanging out with Joe that she totally forgot about her deadline. She silently prayed that everything was waiting for her in her email box.

She had her article done and was waiting for four more articles to pull her section of the paper together. She had one article sitting in her email that was well written, one that

# An Unfinished Story

contained grammatical errors, sentence fragments, and was completely disorganized, one email saying that Susanna quit and would not be continuing with the job, and one email apologizing that the deadline wasn't met. She also had an email from Mark asking her where her section was, then a second email saying he needed to meet with her first thing on Tuesday. Joanie sat there, staring at the screen, not really understanding the magnitude of what just happened.

Panic quickly set into Joanie. Anger was boiling from her toes up to her ears. Frustration, because she had no control over these people, threatened the tears to fall. What was she going to do? She had two articles. Two. Two out of five, which meant that she was unable to rally her team and lead the way she needed. At this time, the paper was busily being printed without her section. She immediately emailed Mark apologizing for her lack of leadership. She agreed to meet with him on Tuesday morning, which meant that she had to leave tomorrow. Joanie knew she was going to get fired. No more job meant no more money. Her thoughts started to spiral out of control. If she was fired, how was she going to get another job? How was she going to pay her rent? She picked up the closest item she could find, which happened to be a teacup and threw it at the wall. It shattered into pieces of all sizes and the tears finally escaped down her cheeks like a waterfall. Joanie instantly felt guilty and promised that she would give Carly money to replace the teacup when she saw her next.

She couldn't fall back asleep and was up and out of bed by 4:30 am. Joanie watched the sun rise over the ocean. The rhythmic slap of the water against the rocks put her at peace and released some of her anxiety. She walked the coast until the rising sun beat down on her shoulders and Joanie feared she got sunburned. The salt air filled her body with relief and the quiet cleared her cloudy mind.

Walking back to the carriage house, she saw Joe in the kitchen window. Joanie knocked on the door to see if he needed any help. She needed to keep busy to keep her upcoming termination out of her mind. "Hey Joe," Joanie called out as she opened the door.

"Oh, hi!" Joe exclaimed. "I am drowning in here. Please save me. The pancakes are burning, I don't have enough burners for the sausage and bacon, all the dishes are dirty, and I ran out of wheat bread."

Joanie giggled, "Okay, okay, let me help. You have twenty five minutes until breakfast. We can do this!" She grabbed an apron and got to work. "Where is Carly? I thought she would be back by now," Joanie asked.

Joe hesitated before responding, "Her mother passed away last night, Joanie. I was supposed to be working this weekend but because she needed help and we are family, I was able to take a few days off. I have to go back to work Wednesday and am basically working seven days straight. Hopefully that is enough time for Carly to return home. If not, we will have to figure something out. Maybe close the inn for a week or so until after things smooth over."

Joanie felt the tears piling behind her eyes making it hard to see. She was a mess emotionally, and couldn't handle any more pain, even if it wasn't her own. She blindly flipped the pancakes onto the plate and buttered the toast in silence. She gave Joe a one armed hug because she felt a hug would be the appropriate response but didn't feel that she knew him well enough to give him a two armed embrace.

They worked in silence for the rest of breakfast and served the guests with smiles on their faces. As they were cleaning up, Joe asked, "Hey, I wanted to talk about yesterday. Why did you leave so suddenly?"

Joanie sighed. She did not feel strong enough to have this conversation right now. Seeing as how her job and adventure on Block Island were likely over, she decided to be honest with him. "Joe, I like you. I enjoy spending time with you and I enjoy learning about you, but I need to tell you something. My last serious boyfriend was when I was in college and it didn't end well. I felt so good with you yesterday and it scared the crap out of me. My feelings are unchartered territory and

## An Unfinished Story

it overwhelms me. So I did what I always do when things get hard. I left to clear my head. I'm sorry if that hurt you."

Joe smiled at her. "I hope you don't take this the wrong way," he started, "but right now we are friends who enjoy spending time together. I don't like labels and I barely know you, but I want to get to know you more. And if being friends leads to something more than I think we should explore it. No pressure. Just friends," he added, "for now."

Joanie sighed again deeply. "Well, unfortunately, I think I am getting fired, so I don't know how much more time we can spend together," Joanie was so frustrated that she was crying again. She had never been fired from a job and had been at this job for fifteen years. Her life path was completely out of whack.

Joe placed his hands on her chin and cheeks and wiped the tears with his thumb. "Please don't cry. Please don't be sad," he whispered. He held her against his broad chest as she sobbed into his shirt pocket.

They decided to spend the day together because Joanie didn't want to be alone with her thoughts and Joe was developing a deep care for Joanie. They went out for lunch, walked the beach, and sat under the trees talking. Joanie felt sad to be leaving but knew she had to find a job quickly. For today, she tried her hardest to enjoy every moment of this beautiful island before having to go back to her reality.

# Chapter 13

"Metal or wood?" the representative from the funeral home asked.

Carly looked around the room, noticing the antique lamps that just faintly produced a glow on the fancy, Victorian furniture. Carly internally criticized their choice of white cushions on the high back chairs and low lying couch. White was a terrible color. It would never be able to hide the tears and sorrow that were shed on a nightly basis when the building was open. Carly thought about funeral homes and how something you experienced a handful of times was intended to provide comfort but only provided confusion and internal chaos.

The man looked at Carly waiting for an answer. "You know, white is a terrible color for sad people," she sputtered.

"I'm sorry?" the man asked. Carly missed his name. She couldn't even remember if he had told her. Maybe he didn't. Maybe he had a generic name, like Dan, or maybe he had a posh, sophisticated name, like Everett. Carly looked at his bushy eyebrows, slicked back hair, and round glasses. He wore a pinstriped suit, square toed shoes, and narrow, striped tie, which somehow fit the decor of the funeral home. She wondered if the owners of the funeral home demanded that Everett dress the part to sell the casket.

"The furniture," Carly started. "White doesn't hide anything. Black or grey would be much more fitting."

Everett cleared his throat. "I will let the owner know." He cleared his throat again. "Now, for the casket. Would you prefer wood? Or would you prefer metal?"

## An Unfinished Story

Carly had no idea what her mom wanted. Actually, she thought her mother would have been more organized for her final resting place, but the dementia certainly interfered with her ability to get her thoughts down on paper. Carly was always so busy with the inn and her mother seemed so healthy, it never seemed to be a priority to find out the details about her death wishes.

"I have ten grand for everything. The casket, the flowers, the reception, and the burial. Give me the nicest, most respectable casket you can give me for 5,000 dollars. The most I can pay for your funeral home and the casket is 8,000. I refuse to take out a line of credit to bury my mother. Honestly, I just want to get this over with so whatever you can do to help me NOT make decisions is perfect for me." Carly's voice cracked and tears filled her eyes. She willed them away. She hoped she didn't sound noncommittal but there were too many choices for a single night that would wrap itself up into eternity.

Everett cleared his throat again and flipped through the demonstration book that was sitting in between the two of them on the couch. He opened the first page and gave her two options for the casket shape. Carly picked the style that resembled her mother. He turned the page and offered two options for fabric. Carly picked red because it was her mother's favorite color. He turned the page and offered two options for presentation of the body. Carly chose the cheaper option because her mother never owned a single lipstick. She never saw the sense in spending money to get her hair colored or nails done, even in her old age. They carried on in this manner until the back cover was closed over the contents and the casket and arrangements were complete.

Carly smiled at Everett and gave thanks for working with her requests. She pulled out her checkbook and paid a deposit for the wake, like it was an event that everyone was dying to attend. She burst out laughing at the irony of her thoughts. "See you Friday," Everett said and he held open the door so Carly could go home and unpack her mother's clothes.

The Willowside was shut down for the week due to a death in the family. Unfortunately the inn was full for the week but Carly couldn't worry right now. Her head was filled with a to-do list that was growing by the second. Call the relatives, find pictures, make a collage, pick out flowers, pick out mass cards, pick out the readings for the service, pick out an outfit for the wake....she wrote it all down and told herself that it would be done by Wednesday.

Carly flipped through her mother's address book and searched for family members. Her mother didn't have any living siblings, but did have nieces and nephews scattered throughout New England. She didn't even know who was family, who were friends, and who were previous guests at The Willowside Inn. Carly decided to go through the Rolodex and start with who she knew. She called her cousins in Rhode Island, Massachusetts, and Maine, and told them to tell everyone who may have known her mother or would want to say goodbye. She also told them that the obituary would be posted the next day and she would forward it to them so they could forward it to their families and mutual friends. The obituary was going into the local paper on Block Island as well as the paper for Southeastern Connecticut. Carly thought maybe the nurse's and CNA's who had gotten to know Ruth over the years would like to come as well.

It was good having her list of things to do because it forced her to set her emotions aside and work through the pain. Joe came over and helped go through the many photo albums Carly had pulled up from the basement. He pulled candid snapshots that captured life as it was occuring. Carly thought that when she died, her collage would be full of selfies, with fake surprise, fake happiness, and fake confusion littering the backdrop. Carly loved that the photos Joe picked out were honest, raw, and exhilarating. The photos encompassed the many emotions of Ruth and were perfect for her celebration of life.

## An Unfinished Story

Carly's parents were going to be buried together after nine long years apart. Knowing that they would be reunited, even if only in death, gave Carly comfort. Her mother was the highlight of her father's life. It was obvious in his smile, his eyes, and his stories. Although Carly's parents were older than most when she was growing up, she always recognized the love they had for each other and when her father died, her mother's heart was broken.

To celebrate her mother's life, Carly decided to watch The Wizard of Oz. They watched that movie every year together and even dressed up as Dorothy, Witch Glinda, and the Wizard for Halloween when Carly was six. She used her favorite stuffed animal, a black dog as Toto, and placed him in an old Easter basket. Carly poured herself a glass of wine, cozied up on the couch, grabbed her mother's afgan from the nursing home and fell into the Wonderful World of Oz, where everyone had a happy ending despite the conflict and controversies.

*********************************************************************
********************************

The silence was deafening. Joanie stared at her lap, her fingers intertwined into each other and squeezing into each other until all her knuckles cracked. She looked at the clock knowing that her meeting with Mark was supposed to start four minutes ago. She could feel the lump in her throat get bigger and threaten to cut off her airway. The air conditioner was not nearly cool enough and the beads of sweat were slowly saturating her hair line. She heard footsteps in the hallway and her heartbeat raced suddenly.

Joanie looked over her shoulder and saw the door knob turn and the hinges creak open. She made eye contact with Mark and tried to give him her most apologetic eyes. She pursed her lips in anticipation. She truly was sorry that her team didn't come through for her. She was sorry that she forgot to send in her section. She was sorry that she let him down. She was also praying for a miracle, that maybe, just possibly, Mark would overlook her incompetence and give her another chance.

Mark nodded. "Joanie," he declared in greeting. Joanie gave him a weak smile. She wanted to blurt out her apologies, but bit her tongue, waiting to be spoken to first. She decided she would wait until the questions were asked, and only answer the questions, because when she started talking, she had a hard time stopping, especially when so much of her life depended on this conversation. She didn't want to look back in an hour, replaying every conversational turn and analyzing how the outcome could have changed had she just said something different. So instead, she waited.

Mark sat at his desk, placed his chin on his fisted hand, and said, "So, how is your summer assignment going?" Joanie was dumbfounded by his question and her mouth dropped open. Of all opening statements, she was not prepared for this one. Was he serious? Was he being sarcastic? Was he being snide? She couldn't read his facial expressions or tone of voice. He asked her as if he were asking how her summer vacation was.

"Um," Joanie began, "the assignment itself has been going well. The rallying of the troops within my department has been tough." She decided honesty was best at this point.

"Your first two articles were great. The last one, I never got to see. It seemed that the printer somehow forgot to include your article. They actually forgot to include your entire section. Isn't that strange?" Mark was pressing her for information in a passive aggressive way and she was buckling under the accusation that was never spoken. She was the reason the entire section was not printed. She was the reason they were getting negative feedback from the public. She was the reason why if they were going to be fired, it was going to happen sooner than later.

"Mark, I am so incredibly sorry. It was my fault that the section was not turned in on time, but even if it had been turned in, there would have been two out of five articles printed. Most of the reporters for the Lifestyle section either

# An Unfinished Story

didn't turn in their assignment or they turned in crap full of grammatical errors and fluff. Yes, it is my fault that the section was not printed but you would have been disappointed either way."

Mark leaned back in his chair stretching his legs out. He folded his hands and placed them on his now protruding belly. "Joanie, we have gotten emails, PeoplePlace posts, and negative reviews for the past 48 hours. People want a refund because their paper was not complete. I am getting pushback from the owners who are getting pushback from the new company. If there was ever a good time to screw up, this was not it." Mark rubbed his eyes with his thumb and forefinger. "Do you want an Advil?" he offered, while popping the top.

Joanie quietly nodded and held out her hand. "What can I do to help the situation?"

Mark sat there, quietly. "I am sorry, Joanie, but we have to let you go. Your assignment has officially been terminated."

Joanie sat there for twenty seconds, just staring at the clock on the wall. It had been four minutes since he walked in the door. A total of eight minutes and her job was gone. Poof! Popped like an overinflated balloon. What was she going to do? She didn't have a job, she had no money, she couldn't even get a roommate because she was living in a one bedroom apartment.

She quickly stood up and grabbed her bag. She threw it over her shoulder and choked back the tears that were sitting in the back of her throat. "Thank you for your time," she whispered.

"Whenever you need a letter of recommendation, please let me know!" Mark called out as Joanie calmly walked out the door. As soon as she was out of his line of vision, she ran down the hall ignoring all of her colleagues staring into her soul. She aggressively pushed open the stairwell door and ran as quickly as she could down the flight of stairs and out into the open air.

She didn't allow herself to cry until she was curled up on her bed with the curtains drawn, and the lights off. The sound of trucks accelerating and cars honking wafted through her open windows. There was no one except her parents who could help her. There was no way Joanie was going to go to them for help.

Joanie took the next two days to apply to jobs. She analyzed her bank account and realized she had approximately one month of savings to get her through, as long as she continued to eat pasta, cereal, and frozen vegetables for all meals of the day. She put a listing out on the community PeoplePlace page looking for a roommate and a job. Her lease was month to month so if she found a place that needed a roommate she could always terminate her lease and move into an 8X8 foot prison cell. It wasn't what she wanted but if she wasn't able to pay her bills, would she really have a choice?

She applied for local delivery jobs, such as Uber, Lyft, pizza places, restaurants, and retail. She had no experience with any of those businesses but knew she could learn if she needed. The problem was that she lived in a high cost area and the rent was astronomical. She thought about applying for jobs all over the country and just starting over. Finding a place for cheap and looking at life from a different perspective. Maybe if she ditched all her plans, whatever path she chose would be the right path to take.

Joanie knew that if she stayed home, didn't get dressed, watched tv all day, and kept all the lights off, depression and anxiety would take over. She had to stay busy, no matter how menial it felt, or else she would get trapped into the mundane cycle of feeling sorry for herself and feeling guilty for all she didn't do.

Friday morning she woke up and knew that she couldn't stay home one more day. She had to go somewhere. The search for apartments and roommates and jobs were depleted and now she would just wait. She told herself that if nothing came up by the end of the month, she would scamper back to her parents with her tail between her legs. Her parents weren't exactly encouraging with her life choices.

## An Unfinished Story

They couldn't understand why she never had a serious relationship, why her maternal instinct to procreate never pushed her to marrying, or why she wanted to live in a city. Joanie knew that going home would be subjecting herself to hearing about how her life could have been different had she just listened to them, all those years ago, and she didn't want to do it.

She felt like she was mourning the loss of her job, the loss of her life, and the loss of the security and predictability in her life. Anger was the first step in the grieving process, and Joanie was pissed. She couldn't believe that her team let her down. Yes, she forgot to send in what she had, but even if she had remembered, she probably still would have been fired for not sending in the entire section. She knew that Mark let her go to save himself from the same future and that made her blood boil. She was just a pawn in the game of corporate life, and she had no control or say in the outcome.

Joanie grabbed her duffle bag and threw in a few changes of clothes. She thought that maybe if she were near the ocean waves, clarity would transpire within herself. She hopped into her car and drove to the Port Judith Block Island Ferry. Being around nature and people who didn't know the state of her life might give her time to process, troubleshoot, and figure out what to do next. She had nothing else to do, right? No job and no commitments. It was time to stop the chaos within her life and grab a hold of her future.

# Chapter 14

Carly's kitchen was filled with food. Her counters were littered with fresh fruit platters, cheesecake, strawberry shortcake, and homemade cookies. Her refrigerator was stuffed with tuna casserole, lasagna, and spaghetti and meatballs. Her sink was overflowing with dirty dishes from when neighbors and friends would stop by bringing food and leaving with a stomach full of hot tea or coffee. Her living room smelled like a funeral home, with arrangements and vases shoved into every corner. Carly looked around, felt the panic rise in her belly, and ran to the bathroom to relieve herself from the chaos within her.

When she stepped back in the living room, she saw Joe sitting quietly on the couch. "I came to help. What do you need?"

Carly felt gratitude toward Joe and everything he had done for her over the past two weeks. She gave him a hug and the tears were immediately released. She sobbed into his shoulder, not caring that his argyle sweater was getting damp. She pulled herself back, wiped her eyes, and said, "The wake starts at 4:30. We need to be there by 4:00. I have to take a shower. Would you mind doing something with these flowers and all this food? It's literally making me sick." Joe nodded and started gathering the vases.

"I'll bring these flowers over to the funeral home. I'll see you there at 4." Carly smiled, put her hands together like she was praying and thanked him.

Around 3:30 she was in the kitchen distributing the last of the dirty dishes into the dishwasher. The door swung open

## An Unfinished Story

and Carly heard a familiar voice, "Hey Carly!" Carly turned and saw Joanie, scanning the state of the kitchen and the state of Carly. Carly was wearing a black A-line dress, black pumps, and black beaded jewelry. Joanie stood there, awkwardly, as she put two and two together.

Joanie felt like such an idiot, not realizing that there was a funeral happening this weekend. She was such a horrible friend, so wrapped up in her own drama, that she didn't even think about what was happening here.

Joanie slowly walked toward Carly, unsure how to proceed. Should she hug her? Say sorry? Suddenly, Joanie stopped at the end of the countertop, "I am so sorry about your mother," she said sincerely. Carly's eyes filled with tears again. It was a never ending supply of tears that had been building since the last time she cried, nine years ago when John returned to Maine never to come back. Carly's shoulders slumped down and she buried her chin into her chest, her shoulders silently heaving.

Joanie put her arms around her and held her for a few moments, wondering how much longer she had to stay in the kitchen. Joanie was "shhh"ing into Carly's hair, waiting for the sobs to dissipate. Joanie pulled away from Carly, looked directly into her eyes, and said, "I need to go get dressed. Leave me the address and I will meet you over there." No one had to know that Joanie completely forgot. It was dumb luck that she showed up on the right day, but at least her friend wouldn't feel so alone.

"Thank you," Carly said as she proceeded to write out the name of the funeral home.

That evening was a blur. Carly's mother was laid out wearing her favorite slacks and sweater. Carly dressed her in her wedding band, her great grandmother's pearls, and a bracelet Carly made as a kid that her mother never threw away. Carly found the bracelet fifteen years later when looking for her mom's diamond bracelet for a wedding she was attending. She asked Ruth about the homemade bracelet and her mom said, "When I look at that, I think back to when you were a little girl and I was your world." She said it with sadness in her voice, which made Carly sad. It was true. Carly had grown up and they had grown apart. All Carly wanted was to get away from her family and her home but fate eventually stepped in and brought her back. This bracelet obviously left an impression on her mother and left her with happier thoughts so Carly placed it around her mother's wrist for the wake and burial.

People from Connecticut showed up to pay their respects in large groups. A wave of CNA's walked through and then a wave of nurses came though. Carly was the only person in the receiving line next to the casket because her father and all her aunts and uncles had passed previously. She felt isolated and alone and completely out of place with no one to lean on in the receiving line. There were only so many "I am sorry" phrases she could hear in one night.

Her cousins from all over New England showed up also. Carly felt terrible that she had a bed and breakfast and refused to allow anyone to stay with her during this time of mourning. The idea of having to keep a house clean while preparing for the services, while mourning the loss of her mother was too much for her emotional and mental state to handle. She didn't want anyone to see her break down in tears because she happened to pull a mug out of the cupboard that her mother drank her tea out of daily. The pain and realization that both of her parents were gone was too much for Carly to handle with an audience.

At the end of the night, the funeral home was emptying out and only a few family members remained. Joanie stood with Joe as he chatted with their cousins from Maine. Joe probably hadn't seen them in twenty years, but it appeared they were chatting and laughing like old times. Carly sat down in a black padded chair in front of the casket and stared at her mother. She looked so strange. Her face was powdery and cakey, her hair was overdone, and her lips were wrinkled and brittle looking. Carly hated open caskets because it painted a fake picture of a person she loved. Carly knew that others wouldn't

## An Unfinished Story

feel closure without saying goodbye unless they could see her body one last time.

"Is this seat taken?" a deep voice asked. Carly wiped her eyes and shook her head no. She continued to stare at the casket and sighed deeply. "I am so sorry for your loss," the voice continued.

Carly turned and saw the familiar kind eyes, the rough hands, and the long legs. "John," she whispered.

"Hi," he whispered back, "I am so sorry to hear about your mother,"

Carly couldn't take her eyes off him. "What are you doing here?" she asked. "How did you know?" She couldn't take her eyes away from his brown, deep, caring eyes. They were just as she remembered but older. There were more lines and more gray hair but Carly recognized him immediately and felt her heart swell with memories.

"I bumped into your cousin Michael at the fish market. He asked if we had spoken recently, and I told him a little bit here and there. He asked if I knew about your mom. When I said, 'no', he told me what happened. I am really sorry."

Carly nodded. She looked over at Joe and Joanie chatting with Michael and his wife, Gloria. Michael was much older than Carly so they were never really close as kids and definitely weren't close as adults. She forgot that Michael lived in Maine and didn't ever think that he knew John. Of course they worked in the same type of industry and Maine is fairly small, so it now made sense that they would have bumped into each other.

"I would have told you," Carly responded, "but I was so overwhelmed with how quickly she passed and how much I had to do to get ready for her services, I completely forgot. Thank you for coming."

John looked the same but older and wiser. His beard was peppered with white, his eyes were decorated with fine lines from years of the rough surf on his skin, and he had put on some weight since the last time they saw each other. He looked more confident in his skin. He looked comfortable and

Carly had a sudden urge to wrap her arms around him and feel his warmth emanate into her body.

They sat there, chatting like old times about Maine, Carly's current life, John's current life, and old memories. It felt normal and comforting to talk about something other than death and loss.

Eventually the funeral home emptied out and all that remained were Joe, Joanie, John, and Carly. Michael and Gloria left to grab dinner and told John they would meet him back at the inn. Not Carly's inn, but an inn solely used for people traveling for funerals. The inn was adjacent to the funeral home and was currently filled with Carly's long lost family whom she didn't remember nor recognize. Joe recognized John as Carly's ex-boyfriend but couldn't recall the details. He whispered into Joanie's ear and they excused themselves. Joe leaned into Carly and said, "Call me if you need anything." Suddenly, he was feeling protective of her emotions.

Carly invited John back to her house so they could continue to catch up and remember what they had and wonder why they allowed it to end. Carly was exhausted mentally and emotionally but needed a mental break from the turmoil she was experiencing on the inside. John's kindness and familiarity was all Carly needed to make it through the night.

# Chapter 15

Joanie rolled over and looked around the room. The shades were drawn, the sunlight was diffused through the curtains, and her clothes were strewn on the floor. Next to her lay a man, his eyes closed, his hair ruffled, and his lean arms outstretched over his head. Joanie wondered what he was dreaming about and if he was dreaming about her.

The previous twenty four hours was a whirlwind that she hadn't quite processed yet. The spur of the moment trip back to the island, as if it was calling her to bring her peace, distracted her from the paper. The shock of walking into Carly's kitchen and seeing the abundance of food surrounding her and the quick trip to find something presentable to wear to the wake made her realize just how much she cared for Carly. Her evening with Joe was completely out of character for her but Joanie decided that her whole life up until that point may have been a charade.

In her previous life, she never would have returned to a man's home, especially a man she didn't really know. Joanie realized how little she actually knew about Joe. Carly shared snippets of information about his leaving and returning to the island and Joe shared snippets of information about his career and his family, but other than that, Joanie knew nothing.

She looked at her watch. The funeral services were starting in three hours, and Joe was a pallbearer. They had to get moving. Joanie quietly climbed out of bed and retrieved Joe's T-shirt, which was given to her as a giant nightshirt. She quietly walked out of the bedroom, into the living room, and

## An Unfinished Story

into the kitchen for some much needed coffee. As the coffee was brewing, Joanie checked out her surroundings, looking for signs of a secret that would bring her back to reality. Could she find signs of a wife, an ex-wife, a girlfriend, or a kid? Everything looked like what you would picture from a bachelor pad. Old sofa with uneven and well used cushions, a television sitting on a night stand from the 1990's, a two person pub table, and a fridge full of beer. Joanie decided this place looked like it belonged to a lonely single man, not a man who may have a woman or child over for Sunday night dinner.

Joanie shook Joe and whispered, "Morning, sunshine. Funeral services start in three hours. Time to get up." Joe moaned and rolled to face her. He smiled at her with his eyes still closed. "Morning, Beautiful," he said in a raspy voice. Joanie leaned down and kissed him on the forehead. "Coffee?" she asked, handing him her cup. He sat up in his bed and took a sip from her mug.

"I need to get back so I can get ready. Would you mind driving me?" Joe nodded, stretched, and grabbed his keys. They agreed he would pick her up thirty minutes before the funeral. Joanie poured her coffee into a to-go cup and looked around one last time. She still couldn't believe she allowed herself to sleep at a man's house that she didn't even know.

When she got back to the carriage house, she called her sister. The past few days had been a whirlwind of activity and a whirlwind of emotion. She experienced happiness, fatigue, anxiety, frustration, fear, sadness, and anger. She kept her drama to herself because she didn't want to interfere with the process Carly and her family were going through. It had been a few days since she sat down with Mark and her world was flipped on its lid. That moment felt like a lifetime ago.

Seeing Carly at the wake in such pain made her heart hurt. Joanie realized that Carly was more than a roommate or a landlord. She was a friend and the only friend Joanie really had. That realization made her miss her sister even more, especially during this chaotic time in her life.

Erica Haraldsen

Joanie had no direction. She had no idea what tomorrow was going to bring, let alone next month or next year. Instead of feeling sorry for herself, she decided to feel freedom. Sure, she was broke, had an apartment she wouldn't be able to afford, and no job, but she was free to start over. Joanie wasn't sure where this newfound attitude and knowledge came from, but she decided to embrace it. Maybe it was because she felt her heart melting whenever she was with Joe. Maybe it was because she never had a desire to be with someone, but she was getting older, and she found her mind continuously wandering to what Joe was doing, wearing, or experiencing. Or better yet, what they would experience together.

Maria's phone rang three times. Joanie expected it to go to voicemail, but Maria picked up, slightly out of breath. "Hey Joanie!" Maria gasped into the phone.

"Hey. Are you okay? Did I wake you?" Joanie looked at her watch. Whoops. 7:30 am on a Saturday was way too early.

"Nah, I was just exercising. Is everything okay? I decided to get up early this morning and go for a run on the beach. It's beautiful today!"

Joanie looked out the living room window and noticed the blue sky and the magenta and lavender flowers in front of the house. The salt air was traveling with the breeze and the birds were chirping in the tree in between the carriage house and the main inn. It certainly was a beautiful day. "Yeah, yeah, everything is fine. I just wanted to talk to you about something."

"Let me guess!" Maria started. "Mom and dad are coming for a surprise visit," she giggled. "Or, you got a dog! Or you have a boyfriend!" Maria was certainly full of energy this morning, Joanie thought.

"Well...kind of. Do you want the good news or the bad news?" Joanied asked.

"Oh shit. There's bad news? I am going to go with bad news first," Maria said without skipping a beat. Joanie

## An Unfinished Story

imagined her jogging on the beach, kicking sand behind her while speaking to Joanie on speakerphone.

"Yeah. I got fired." Joanie said definitively.

"You what?!" Maria's voice elevated an octave as she screeched into the phone. It was evident that Maria stopped mid stride.

"Yeah, I screwed up. It wasn't entirely my fault. We were being bought out. I'm sure you saw on the news. We had until August 1st to prove ourselves to the new company, otherwise we would be let go. Well, my team under me jumped ship without telling me and just didn't turn in their articles. So when everything was due, there was kind of an emergency here, on Block Island, and I forgot to turn in what I had. And the paper was printed without our section." Joanie spoke quickly.

"Wow!" Maria exclaimed.

"Yeah, so even though no one did their work---because I didn't turn in the section on time, I took the hit for everyone," Joanie paused, expecting a reaction, but nothing came. She continued, "So I got fired."

There was a few seconds delay, and Joanie imagined Maria transitioning from stopping to jogging. "Shit, Joanie, what are you going to do?"

"I have no idea! At first I was upset because I thought it was unfair that I got in trouble even though no one did the work, but I kind of feel relieved. Like, this is an opportunity to find myself. Recreate myself. Figure out what I want for my life, now that I am almost forty, kidless, and husbandless."

"Yeah, you definitely don't sound sad about it. Does Mom and Dad know?" Maria asked.

"No! And you can't tell them. At least not until I have a plan. Promise me, Maria."

"Yeah, yeah, your secret is safe with me. But they are coming for Thanksgiving, so you better have it straightened out by then. You know I can't lie to their face." Maria said.

"Promise. Give me a month. I will have a plan. Now, are you ready for the good news?" Joanie asked with a grin on her face.

"Well, you just got fired. Anything would be good news compared to that," Maria exhaled into the phone. Joanie could tell she was cooling down from her vigorous exercise routine.

"I met a guy!!" Joanie shrieked into the phone. She felt like she was in 7th grade again. She wasn't sure if she should tell anyone because it was so new and there was a chance that Joe didn't feel any similar emotions that she was feeling.

Maria shrieked into the phone with her. "Tell me tell me tell me!" it sounded like she was jumping up and down.

Joanie told her how they met, how they took care of the inn together, how they spent time on the beach and at his house, and how wonderful he made her feel. She told her that she was going to spend some time on the island to figure out her future. She and Carly had agreed until the end of August and Joanie was praying that the offer still stood. That deadline gave her three weeks to figure out her next move.

Joanie told Maria she had to run because she had to get ready for the funeral. She promised Maria that she would ask Carly if her and Chris could come up for a weekend to spend some time with her. Life was so unpredictable. Joanie needed her sister.

\*\*\*\*\*\*\*\*\*\*\*\*\*\*\*\*\*\*\*\*\*\*\*\*\*\*\*\*\*\*\*\*\*\*\*\*\*\*\*\*\*\*\*\*\*\*\*\*\*\*\*\*\*\*\*\*\*\*\*\*\*\*\*\*\*\*\*\*\*\*\*\*\*\*\*\*\*\*\*\*\*\*\*\*\*\*\*\*\*\*\*\*\*

The funeral was an absolute blur. Carly spent the entire ceremony with tears streaming down her face and sobs escaping from her lips. She felt so alone and isolated, sitting in the front row of the pew with aunts, uncles, and cousins she hadn't seen in over two decades. When her parents bought the inn, they basically became a slave to Block Island, and Carly became a slave by default. Her closest family lived hours away, so Christmas, Thanksgiving, and holidays were spent alone.

## An Unfinished Story

Carly sat next to Joe, watching the priest's lips move but not hearing or comprehending a word. Her brain kept jumping around, like someone trying to catch a radio station in tune, but everytime the signal cleared, it became staticy again. Memories from her childhood, from her dad's funeral, and from the nursing home all collided within her brain, fighting for her attention. Eventually her brain became numb and the memories subsided. Instead, Carly scraped the paint off her fingernails, which was a habit she started when she was a teen.

People that she had never met and never even heard of before hugged her awkwardly and softly. Many were from the nursing home, many were long lost relatives, and many were old guests at the inn who eventually became friends of her parents. Carly was thankful for the familiar faces of people from the island that came out to support her. When she was stuck conversing with a stranger and ultimately comforting the random man or woman in front of her, she would make eye contact with a familiar face and her heart would relax. *Just two more hours* she told herself, over and over.

After the service, they all traveled to the local cemetery to the place where Carly's father was buried. Carly hadn't been to her father's headstone in years, and she mentally apologized for being such a terrible daughter. She felt comforted knowing that her mother was finally back with her father. Their love, support, and compassion for each other was something Carly always admired.

She felt a hand on the small of her back and turned to see John, standing behind her in a long, black trench coat. Carly smiled. She knew this was all he had and he was trying to look his best, but he looked silly standing in such a heavy outer garment in the middle of August. It wasn't even raining. Without saying a word, Carly leaned into his broad shoulders and wrapped her arms tightly around his torso. "Thank you," she whispered, looking up into his eyes. "I needed that."

He stood by her side for the remainder of the burial and allowed her to lean on him when feeling weak, alone, confused, or sad. They had a lot to talk about, but now was not the place. Carly felt at ease next to him. His warm body was erasing the numbness within her and his strength was giving her the energy to remain upright and participate in random conversations with strangers. "Please don't leave me," Carly said. "I need you here." John nodded and stayed by her side for the rest of the day.

At the reception afterward, a crowd of about 40 people stayed. The reception was at The Willowside Inn because that seemed the most affordable and the most appropriate since Carly's parents dedicated so much of their life to that place. Fortunately, the townspeople came together and dropped off various potluck items throughout the morning so food was plentiful. The weather held out and the sun remained shining. Carly saw one single dragonfly land on the banister of the porch where she was sitting. It sat there for about 45 seconds, just resting and looking at her. Carly couldn't help but think it was her mom coming to visit. *I love you Mom,* Carly whispered to the dragonfly. After her words, it flew away and Carly watched until it could no longer be seen.

She felt much more comfortable and at ease at The Willowside. This was where she grew up. If people didn't like the food, they could leave or if they didn't like the weather, they could leave. When everyone left, she would drink a bottle of wine by herself, crash on the couch, and forget that this was her life.

Joanie, Joe, and John stayed the entire day, which turned into evening, which turned into night. All the other guests slowly dissipated, leaving to catch the last ferry back to the mainland, heading home, or headed to the inn next to the funeral home. The four of them sat outside on the open farmer's porch looking into the fields. Lightning bugs were sporadically putting on a light show for them to enjoy. The temperature was still warm but the mugginess had gone.

"Carly, do you remember trying to catch lightning bugs when we were kids?" Joe asked, staring into the dark night.

## An Unfinished Story

Carly smiled. "I don't remember catching them, I remember you terrorizing me with them."

"Wait a minute....tell me the story!" John chided.

Joe laughed and pulled Joanie close to him. "I was five years older than Carly, so when she was seven, I was twelve. Our parents would have dinner together a few times a month, and when it was warm, we would eat outside. I was a horrible cousin and thought it would be funny to scare Carly. I captured all the lightning bugs I could find and trapped them in a jar. I told Carly that if the bugs lit up, it meant that they were ghosts trying to enter our world and kill us."

"Yeah!" Carly interrupted, "And of course I didn't believe him, and then he unscrewed to cap and only had his hand blocking the opening! He said, 'These are all ghosts and the more they light up the more they are trying to get out. The first person they touch is whose body they will take over' and then he moved his hand and threw the bugs on me!" Carly started laughing and shaking her head in disbelief at the memory.

Joanie gave Joe a poke in the side. "That is so mean!"

John pulled Carly close and hugged her from behind.

"Yeah, it was mean. I was a mean kid, what can I say. I got in so much trouble for doing that to you! Your parents and my parents took me inside and scolded me for being so cruel. And then they made me write you an apology saying everything I said was a lie."

Carly laughed. "You are the reason why I don't like camping! Too many bugs that want to take over my soul".

They sat outside talking about life, death, childhood and adulthood. Eventually the three friends left Carly alone to think, grieve, or process, while they cleaned up the kitchen. Carly realized that she was 39 years old and officially an orphan. Those words seemed so harsh and unkind for someone so young. No mom, no dad, no brothers or sisters, no husband, no boyfriend, no kids. The feelings of loneliness and isolation wrapped themselves around her and squeezed her tight. She pulled her legs up into her chest on the chair and wrapped her arms around them. The numbness was subsiding and the tears were falling. Carly wished things were different. She was too young to be alone.

She took a sip of her wine and continued to stare into the darkness. Her life had been a series of decisions made to make her parents happy. And now they were gone. As Carly looked back on her choices, she knew that she should have been less bendable and accommodating to their needs. She sacrificed her own life for their dream. Now she was running a bed and breakfast that she didn't even want. The feelings of anger and resentment crashed into the isolation and loneliness and animosity filled her soul. She felt like there were so many opportunities wasted for her to follow her dreams or live the life she intended. Carly looked around and realized how much of the inn was for her parents and how little was for her. Sadness and resentment crashed into her anger and absorbed it. She cried not for her mom, but for the lost opportunity of her past and her future. Carly couldn't handle the mess of emotions within herself anymore. She took another gulp of wine and stumbled into the house to distract herself from her emotions.

# Chapter 16

The day after the funeral, Joanie sauntered into The Willowside to check on Carly. They weren't expecting any guests until the following weekend to allow Carly time to organize herself and the piles and mountains of paperwork her mother left her. "Knock, knock!" Joanie called out through the kitchen door.

"Hey! I'm in here," Carly called from the dining room. Joanie walked in to find piles of papers on every table. Carly was sitting facing the front window staring out into the yard with a hot, piping coffee mug in her hand. She took a sip and didn't move as she continued, "What do you think happens when people die?"

Joanie sat down next to her but didn't want to get too close for fear of making Carly uncomfortable. Carly didn't even acknowledge the movement across the room. "Um. I don't really know. I was raised to believe that good people went to heaven, and I am assuming your mom was good. So she is probably in heaven. I have no reason to believe otherwise. What do you think?"

Carly sat there in silence watching the bumble bees travel from flower to flower. "I don't know," she whispered. She wiped away a tear that fell onto her cheek. "Do you think she is with my dad?"

"Absolutely!" Joanie quickly responded. "I do believe that when a man and woman love each other and give their lives to each other, they are together in life and death. And you were the third part of their heart, so you will one day be with them too."

## An Unfinished Story

Carly looked down at her lap and her shoulders rose and fell rhythmically. "I hope so. I hope my mom in heaven is who my mom was the day they got married. I hope that she isn't the person whose life was robbed by disease. My dad misses her. I just know it."

They watched a dragonfly flutter next to the window, as if paralyzed by hope and sadness. Joanie and Carly sat in silence until the dragonfly disappeared into the horizon. Carly wiped her eyes and returned her gaze to her coffee. Suddenly her stomach turned and she placed the mug on the glass table.

"Are you okay?" Joanie asked, touching Carly's arm. Carly looked over at Joanie. "I mean, I know you aren't okay. Your mom just died. But how are you feeling? Do you need help with anything?" Joanie scanned the room from pile to pile to pile.

"I have been up all night. Every time I closed my eyes, memories from my childhood came crashing into me. One time, my mom taught me how to make my great grandmother's chocolate chip cookies. Another time, my mom took me ice skating in secret because my Dad was afraid I would break my ankle. My mom took me and then bribed me with ice cream not to tell my dad. Another time, I got a horrible haircut and my mom felt so bad, she went out and got the same haircut so I wouldn't feel so bad," Carly giggled remembering how ridiculous they both looked. "I couldn't sleep."

"Your mom sounds like a beautiful person. She raised you and you are a beautiful person too. You were lucky to have her," Joanie soothed.

Carly started crying. "I never acted lucky. I hated that my parents were so much older than my friend's parents. I hated that they could have been my grandparents. I hated that I was stuck at this inn the majority of my childhood and missed out on fun activities because they were too busy taking care of guests. Yes, my mom was a beautiful person, but I was so ungrateful of her love. I was resentful that I didn't have a brother or sister because I was all alone." Joanie passed Carly a tissue and rubbed her arm. She felt slightly awkward, not really knowing Carly and not ever knowing her mom.

"But none of that matters," Joanie guessed. "Your mom and dad knew you loved them. Trust me, none of us had perfect childhoods, but it sounds like your mom tried to make it special when she could. She wouldn't have done those things if she didn't love you. You were her world," Joanie guessed again.

Carly nodded to her reflection in the window. "Thank you for listening." It seemed that the conversational door had just been shut, and Joanie was relieved because she didn't know what to say next. After a few moments, Joanie asked about the paper mountains littered around the room.

"Oh you know, documents from the nursing home, Medicaid and Medicare papers, birth certificate, passport, will, papers from my childhood that probably can be tossed, old bank statements, who knows what else."

"Do you need any help going through it?" Joanie asked, "I would be happy to help."

Carly shook her head, "It's going to take me a while, but I think I can get everything done and situated before the guests arrive next week." She continued to sit, staring out the window.

Joanie made her some fresh hot coffee and breakfast while Carly sat staring out the window. She ran to the grocery store for her to stock up on healthy food that would keep her going through the week. She dumped all the desserts and casseroles that had been sitting in the fridge for days. Slowly, Joanie made herself useful and helped with the inn and helped her new friend mend her broken heart. Carly continued to sit and stare until the sun set and the lightning bugs came out. Then she went to bed.

*****************************************************************
********************************

# An Unfinished Story

The next morning, Carly woke up with the sun shining through her window. The warmth from the sunbeams warmed her soul and motivated her to get out of bed and take a shower. She was so grateful for all Joanie had done yesterday. It seemed to be the little things that completely overwhelmed her and paralyzed her from being her active, organized, in control self. She didn't recall doing anything yesterday. Just sitting and thinking and processing. Separating all those papers was enough for one day, and maybe today would be the day that one or two piles were tackled. She was thankful that Joanie let her sit, without judging her or encouraging her to get up before she was ready.

After a hot, steamy shower, Carly threw on her sweats and a t-shirt before going downstairs. She technically got dressed, which was progress. She could smell coffee and bacon as she approached the landing of the staircase. Carly immediately thought Joanie was in the kitchen cooking food to get her body nourished.

Instead of finding Joanie, she found John, facing the stove with his back to her, wearing her favorite apron, flipping bacon and sausage. Carly must have muttered a noise in her bewilderment and John turned around with a smile on his face. "Good morning! I hope you are hungry!"

"Hi. How did you get in here?" Carly asked, crossing her arms over her braless chest.

"Many moons ago, you gave me a key. I've been holding onto it for years, never really convinced that I would ever see you again." John admitted. "I knew you would be sleeping so I thought I would surprise you."

Carly walked over and gave him a stiff hug. She felt happy to see him but also confused because she didn't know who they were to each other and also kind of annoyed because he let himself in without her knowing. She grabbed her sweatshirt from the couch and threw it over her shirt. Instantly she felt better.

"So how long will you be in town?" Carly asked awkwardly, pulling her hair back into a ponytail.

John looked at her for just enough seconds to make her shift her weight from one leg to the other. She clasped her hands in front of her, quickly crossed her arms, put her hands on her hips, and then sat down to try and calm her anxious limbs. "Actually, I have to head back tomorrow," John said. "I wish it could be longer, but you know how crazy lobster season can get."

John poured her a cup of coffee and asked if she still liked half and half with two sugar cubes. Carly laughed, flattered that he remembered. She nodded and replied, "Only two sugar cubes and one teaspoon half and half. I wouldn't want to throw the proportions off." When Carly and John were living together in Maine, they drank beer at night and coffee during the day. They were broke and couldn't afford to purchase coffee from an actual coffee shop, so they spent an entire day trying different variations of coffee, sweeteners, and dairy products to find THE perfect cup of coffee. Carly found that sugar cubes were a better measurement than loose sugar and it tasted perfect every time two sugar cubes were used.

"Yeah, I thought it was kind of funny that you had sugar cubes in your cabinet and I immediately thought of our coffee days," John said and he plopped two sugar cubes into her mug. Carly smiled feeling nostalgic as the scent of coffee made by John hit her nose.

"Thank you," she smiled. "This is perfect." She took a sip and was suddenly whisked away to their tiny apartment in Portland overlooking the harbor. She could see the boats in the marina, the water lapping against the docks, the restaurants and shops below, and the smell of the city. She felt content and satisfied as she sipped her coffee and ate breakfast that she didn't have to make for once. "I know you have to go tomorrow, but you are always welcome to come back as long as you would like. It would be nice to catch up after all these years," Carly said with a smile.

## An Unfinished Story

Carly and John spent the day together. He told her that his job was to make her feel better and ease her mind from the looming responsibility of going through her mother's estate. He didn't say that in quite so many words exactly, but Carly inferred his message. She was grateful for the companionship during this tedious and burdensome task.

She was going to miss him. She thanked him for his support and for showing up. It was quite a surprise, and she was happy to have him there during this horrible moment in her life. At that, John leaned down, and tenderly kissed her lips. Carly wasn't ready for it and her heart leapt into her throat and her lips tingled. She pulled away and stared into his deep, dark eyes. After a few moments, his eyes showed fear and remorse and then confusion. Carly placed her hands along the back of his head and played with his hair. She pulled him into her and kissed him hard. Her heart exploded and the tears fell from her eyes. She pulled away, wrapped him into a tight hug, and sobbed into his shoulder.

After a few moments, John pulled away, and asked if she was okay. Carly nodded and said, "When you left me, my heart was broken. I don't think I ever allowed myself to grieve. I just picked up the broken pieces, stuffed them deep into my pocket, and never took them out again. I learned how to live with a broken heart. When I kissed you, my feelings went crazy inside my body. Everything I felt toward you...the good, the bad, the great, and the ugly came crashing together. It completely overwhelmed me. I'm sorry." Carly looked down at her hands in her lap, too ashamed to look at John. She was too scared to see the outcome of being so truthful.

John knelt down beside her, grabbed her hands, raised them to his lips and tenderly kissed them. "I'm sorry," he whispered. "I am so sorry." With that, Carly stood up, holding her hands in his and pulled him up with her. She turned away from him and quietly led him up to her bedroom.

*****************************************************************
********************************

Joanie called Joe to ask if he could go for a walk down at the beach. Joe had two more days off for bereavement before having to head back into work. They met near the park bench where they had lunch the day of the newspaper interview. Joanie arrived first, iced coffee in hand, wearing her favorite jean shorts and a white tank top. The island had done her well so far this summer, and her skin had a warm glow to her otherwise pasty skin.

"Hey Beautiful!" a deep voice bellowed from her left. She turned to see Joe walking toward her wearing loose jeans that hung around his hips, black flip flops, and a black t-shirt that advertised a bar in town that was probably given to him at their grand opening. Joanie noticed that his hair was tousled and damp and she wondered if he had just gotten out of the shower.

Joanie stood to greet him and he gave her a gentle peck on the lips. "Hi," she said, looking up to meet his eyes, smiling brightly. "I have to talk to you about something."

A look of concern flashed over his face and she grabbed his hands and pulled him down to the bench next to her. She wrapped her fingers through his and covered the top of his hand with her other hand. She stayed like that, for a few moments, trying to figure out how best to break the news that she was jobless, scared, and alone. "I got fired," she blurted out. No matter how many people she told or how many times she said it, she still felt the same level of shame cover her body. She looked down in embarrassment. At first, she was angry, like, how dare Mark fire her! But now she was just embarrassed. She had been there fifteen years and was part of their family, and yet she was easily discarded like a bag of trash, as if her fifteen years had meant nothing. She had never been fired before.

"I'm so sorry!" Joe said. "What are you going to do?"

Joanie felt tears forming behind her eyes and didn't understand where they were coming from. The thought of having no idea where her future was going was terrifying to her and the fear of screwing up her life worse than she already

## An Unfinished Story

had was driving her emotions. She was afraid to let down her parents, afraid to struggle financially, afraid to make a mistake, and afraid that what she had was the pinnacle of her life. Instead of answering Joe, Joanie leaned into his shoulder before he could see her tears and cried silently. She felt so stupid for losing control of herself.

Joe pulled her back and wiped her tears from her cheekbone with his thumb. "Shhh. It's going to be okay. You're going to be okay." Joanie took a deep breath and tried to compose herself.

"I am so sorry. I don't know why I am crying," she said between giggles. "I feel so stupid. I know I am going to be okay. I just don't know where to go from here. I feel like my life is sitting at a four way intersection and the light is stuck on red, and all the cars are behind me beeping because I am afraid that if I run it, a police officer will pull me over and ticket me for doing the wrong thing."

Joe pulled out his badge and replied, "I promise, I will never pull you over for sitting at a red light." Joanie giggled because her analogy didn't make any sense, but she hoped that Joe understood what she meant. Hell, Joanie didn't even understand her feelings yet. It was obvious that she couldn't articulate them properly.

"No, seriously," Joe responded, "you take as long as you need to figure it out. There is no harm in pausing your life to figure out your next move. It happens all the time in Chess. Think of how long someone can sit before making a move in that game. And the reason why? Because every move has a reaction that can either help or harm them. There is nothing wrong with pausing. Are you heading back to Boston?" There was a glimmer of hope in his question.

"Not yet. I am staying at the carriage house until the end of the month. If I go back, I am going to be thrown back into the hustle and bustle of life and I will probably be forced to make a decision before I am ready. I am here for a few more weeks. I still have to figure out what to do about my apartment, because if I am not getting paid for the next 5 weeks, I can't pay my rent. And I can't tell my parents. They will just say *I told you so* and I refuse to let that happen. Maybe I can find a job helping out somewhere to get some extra cash. I don't know. With everything happening with Carly's mom I haven't even spoken to her, but I will." Everything poured out of her mouth like a waterfall. Joe just sat there, listening. He had no answers for her, because ultimately it was her job to find them herself, but he was a good friend and he cared for Joanie.

They spent the afternoon talking about her job, her qualifications, her experiences, and her dreams. They didn't come to any conclusions, but Joe promised he would ask around and see if she could help out somewhere on the island. She was stuck in a moment of uncertainty, but like life, things could change instantly.

That night she knocked on Carly's door to see if she wanted to grab dinner together. Joanie was exhausted from the constant thinking with Joe and felt that she had to share what was going on in her life. The kitchen door was open ajar so Joanie let herself in after knocking three times on the door loudly. "Carly? Are you home?" Joanie called through the doorway.

Carly sauntered into the kitchen wearing tight jeans, a cute button down blouse, and black flats. Her hair was brushed, her face was glowing, and she looked confident and content. "Joanie! Hey! How are you?" Carly responded with a smile. Joanie could not believe this was the same despondent girl from yesterday who didn't get up from her chair once.

"Wow! You look amazing! Did I interrupt? It looks like you are going out on the town!"

Carly continued to smile, her lips curved up toward her cheekbones. "Oh, no! I had a great day today, hanging out with John, and I feel so much better than I did yesterday! I think all I needed was a hot shower and a good night's sleep." Carly sauntered over to the fridge and poured herself a tall

## An Unfinished Story

glass of orange juice. "Do you want some?" she motioned to Joanie with the orange juice in hand.

Joanie shook her head. She looked into the dining room and saw the numerous piles untouched. Clearly, Carly was able to put her stress and anxiety on the back burner in order to pull herself together. Carly seemed so upbeat and positive in this moment, Joanie knew that this was the perfect time to break the news about her life. She cleared her throat and turned toward Carly. "Can I talk to you about something? It's something that has been on my mind for the past few days." Joanie sat down at the kitchen table and patted the spot next to her to invite Carly to sit down.

"Last week, I was fired." This was the third time she was telling this story, and with every retelling it felt more and more like it wasn't happening to her, but to someone she knew. Everything just spilled out, but this time it was in the correct chronological order and she kept her emotions out of it. "So," Joanie finished, "if you know of anyone who is looking for some extra help, please keep me in mind. In the meantime, I will be applying for jobs back in Boston. I might be here until the end of August or I might leave earlier, depending on what happens with the job situation."

Carly reached over and gave Joanie a big hug. "Hang in there," she said, squeezing Joanie's forearm, "it will get better." It was strange that Carly was comforting Joanie when Joanie was comforting Carly the night before. With that, Carly's phone buzzed and she said, "Hey, I'm sorry to cut this short. I am meeting John for a drink. Can we catch up tomorrow?" And just like that, Joanie was alone in the kitchen, wondering how Carly transitioned from depressed mourner to giddy dater in a matter of minutes. Just as easily, she thought, as me having a job on Tuesday at 9 am and being jobless at 9:30. Life happens and a lot of times you don't see the shift until it is over. It's like a tornado. By the time you hear the siren, it might be touching down on your house while your neighbor's house is pristine and standing. You just never know what life will throw at you.

# Chapter 17

"I don't understand," Carly said to Bob Dryer, her father's attorney. She was holding a piece of paper that had multisyllabic words and acronyms that she couldn't read, let alone understand. The entire document was mumbo-jumbo and Carly needed Bob to translate.

"Your mother is leaving her entire estate to you. Her money, her savings, her assets, and The Willowside Inn. She left you everything but did state that she wants The Willowside Inn to remain in the family for future generations." Bob said.

"Wait, what? How will she know if it stays in the family? I don't have any kids and she is dead." Carly said deadpanly.

"Well, yes. Correct. And it seems that the person who drafted the will knew the legal complexities of that as well. Obviously, in your will, you can break that statement, but your mother intended for it to go to you, debt free."

Carly sat there, anger fuming within her. She continued to feel trapped within her parents expectations. She hadn't even thought about selling The Willowside any time soon, but now that the option to sell was off the table, she felt defeated and frustrated.

"And what happens if I end up selling, for whatever reason? Maybe I need the money, or maybe I want to move, or maybe I need a change? What happens then?" Carly asked quickly.

"Well, if you sell, the proceeds from the sale will be divided up among all the small businesses on Block Island. Your mother and father worked their lives away to make the inn a success and your mother wants to pay it forward to other

## An Unfinished Story

struggling businesses. It's right here," Bob said, pointing to the disclosure. "Unfortunately, because Block Island is so small, the bank, the law office, the real estate offices, and the Town Clerk are all aware of her wishes. I don't know how you would get away with selling and keeping the money if you tried to sell while brushing her final wishes under the rug."

Carly sat there. The color drained from her face. Her anger turned to shock. She couldn't believe her mother could be so vindictive. Carly was an only child with no children. They barely had any family and Carly continued to carry the burden of her parents choices. It seemed so incredibly unfair.

"Thank you, Bob," Carly said, standing abruptly. "I think I have heard enough for one day." With that, she turned on her heel and exited the law office. She needed some time to think.

Carly walked along the beach, listening to the ocean waves lap against the rocky shoreline. She looked around, admiring the beauty of the ocean. The rocky coast, the blue sky, and the unpredictable waves kept her grounded. Carly tried to change her perspective and think of her mother's gift as a blessing. The inn was paid for, she already knew how to run it successfully, and she lived in a place where most people dream of vacationing. Even with the positive thoughts flowing through her mind, the anger and trickery was overpowering her psyche. Carly felt trapped. She had no control of her life and she hadn't had control since she was living in Maine. Everything she did was for her family and this was how she was repaid for her years of service and sacrifice. Carly didn't necessarily want to sell or leave the island, but her lack of choices made her want to get revenge and teach her parents that she was her own person who could make her own decisions, regardless of how they felt.

Carly made it back to the inn while walking in a daze. Her mind, body, and soul felt numb to the news she received. Her anger subsided, and she was filled with a dark, empty void that traveled from her heart to the pit of her stomach. Sitting at the kitchen table was John, Joe, and Joanie, having the last of the tuna casserole Mrs. Pickering brought over to feed Carly while she was grieving.

John got up and gave Carly a kiss. He could see the lack of emotion on her face and the paleness of her skin. He poured her some lemonade and invited her to join them at the table. "Are you okay?" he asked semi-privately, away from the others. Carly nodded feeling the anger bubble up from her stomach to her throat again. There was a rock sitting on her vocal chords daring her to cry.

John gave her a hug and the floodgates opened wildly. Carly couldn't stop the emotions from pouring out of her onto the kitchen table with all of her friends watching. She was crying for the death of her mother, the death of her independence, the death of her freedom, and the bitterness that she didn't even know existed within her soul. Everyone waited uncomfortably for Carly to say the first word. Joanie rubbed her thumb up and down the condensation on her cup. Joe excused himself to go to the bathroom, and John rubbed her back as he pulled her into his chest.

Carly took a deep breath and let out a loud sigh. "You guys, she tricked me. I thought that finally, FINALLY," Carly's voice rose in frustration, "I would be able to leave here and follow my heart and my dreams but I can't. Her will states that the inn goes to me, and any money from the selling of the inn goes to every small business owner on this island. You guys, I came here to help her! I came here because it was best for the family! I stayed here, sacrificing the life I made....WE MADE," she shot a look at John, "in Maine to help her. I paid my dues to support her, and love her, and help her, and THIS is how she pays me? By trapping me into her life with no opportunity to follow my heart, my dreams, and my desires. I cannot believe she was so selfish! And I never even knew. I should have stood up to her a long time ago. I can't believe I was so stupid!" Carly took a sip of her lemonade and stared out the window. Her thoughts were running wildly and quietly in her brain and she couldn't keep anything straight. The whole thing seemed unreal.

## An Unfinished Story

John grabbed an armful of beers and placed them on the table. "This is for you," he handed one to Carly, "and you," he handed one to Joanie, "And us, for being here with you." He handed one to Joe and passed around the bottle opener. "Let's have a beer and figure out what this means."

They sat around the table all night, going over the will and exactly what it said. They talked about Joanie losing her job and what her next move should be. They talked about life back in Maine and opportunities there. They talked and talked and talked until the topics went full circle and an entire twelve-pack of beer was gone. The stress of the night had slowly subsided with each sip of alcohol. They hadn't come to any conclusions, but Carly felt in her heart that no change could be made. John was returning to Portland, Joanie was returning to Boston, and Carly would still be here. Booking reservations, cooking breakfast, and doing laundry on an island where she knew everyone. Even though life wasn't going to change, she at least had one night where she let all her emotions out on the table. She felt better because nothing was left inside. Her soul felt empty.

# Chapter 18

Joanie hustled around the kitchen with a red and white checked apron around her waist. The coffee aroma was wafting into the dining room, the bacon was sizzling, and the pancakes were golden brown. Joanie piled the food on square plates and placed them on a rolling tea cart. She transferred the drinks to the top shelf and grabbed a handful of napkins. Joanie pushed the tea cart into the dining room and found a room full of guests. Some guests she knew and some were strangers. They were all sitting at their tables with their legs crossed and a newspaper outstretched in front of them. No one looked up when Joanie entered. She looked at their newspapers and every person was reading the Lifestyle section.

Joanie shook a bell sitting on the tea cart and all eyes turned to her. She saw Mark, Carly, John, Maria and Chris, and a group of strangers. Joanie didn't recognize any of them. "Hello, everyone! Welcome to breakfast!" Joanie took everyone's order and quickly dispersed the food. She turned around and found Joe, pouring orange juice, apple juice and cranberry juice. He was wearing a red and black checked chef hat that matched Joanie's apron.

As everyone was eating, she could see faint conversations around the room. "She made a change,"; "She left the newspaper,"; "She found happiness in the most unexpected place," were random comments that flowed through the air in Times New Roman font. Joanie read them all as they cascaded around her before disappearing into the ceiling.

## An Unfinished Story

*Joanie tried to talk to Joe about the words she was reading but no sound came out. She roamed around the room to see if she could read the paper, and in big bold letters, she read, "From Media to Hospitality: The Willowside Inn Under New Management". The thoughts and words of all the people eating breakfast swirled until she couldn't see anything but a white fog around her. Everything whipped around her and she screamed in glee. Suddenly, the sound, the words, and the background dropped away and Joanie was left standing alone on the beach. She heard a dog barking in the distance and turned to see flashes of light in the sky. Then everything went black.*

Joanie opened her eyes instantly. Joe was standing over her with his camera in hand. "Sorry, you looked so peaceful and so beautiful when you slept. I didn't want to forget you." Joanie sat upright and grabbed his hands.

"Joe. I got it. I know what to do."

Joe looked at her quizzically. "You want to run away together?" he joked with her.

"No! Yes! Kind of! We...me and you...will take over The Willowside Inn! Carly doesn't have to sell it and you are her family. Her mother's wishes will still be respected but she will be free to live her life! I will have a job. I won't have to leave you and Carly won't have to say good-bye to John! For legal purposes, we can manage the property while she still owns it. She can teach us how to do it. It can't be that hard!" Joanie was talking faster and faster, worried that if she took a breath her idea would vanish.

Joe looked deep into her eyes, trying to ground her. "But I have a job and I love my job," Joe said.

"No problem! I will run the inn and you can be my partner. The person I run to when I need help brainstorming or need help with recipes or when the toilet gets clogged! You will be my sidekick when you are free. Carly will oversee the inn and I will do what she asks. When I need help I will go to you! What do you think?" Joanie jumped out of bed and grabbed her jeans. She quickly brushed her teeth and pulled on her flip flops.

"Where are you going?" Joe asked, still in bed with the blankets all around him.

"To see Carly! This could work, Joe! This could work!" and with that, Joanie ran outside and into the kitchen of the main inn.

Carly and John were embraced in the kitchen. His overnight bag was at his feet and Carly held onto his large frame for three seconds too long. She disengaged from his arms and kissed him gently and longingly on the lips. Joanie turned her eyes away, feeling uncomfortable witnessing such an intimate moment. She knocked on the door behind her to alert them of her presence.

Carly turned toward Joanie to reveal red, puffy eyes and a sad smile. "Hi Joanie," she said emotionless. Joanie raised her hand in a half wave and sat down at the kitchen table.

"John, are you leaving already?" Joanie asked.

"Yeah, my ferry leaves at 10:15. I could only take off a few days of work. This is our busiest fishing time, so I can't leave my lobster boat for much longer. I"m going to get back tonight and start work again tomorrow." Joanie looked at her watch. It was 8:45 and she knew that they could give her at least ten minutes of their time before he had to go. Joanie felt awful for interrupting their private time, but knew that if she didn't share her thoughts now, the excitement would pass and who knows where they would all end up.

"Have a safe trip back. It was really nice meeting you. I can see that you make Carly happy and that makes me happy. She's my only friend here and she deserves to be happy."

"Thanks. It was great meeting you too," John said. There was an awkward silence and Joanie could tell that they wanted her to leave.

"Uh, okay. I promise I won't be here long, but I have to tell you! I have the most perfect idea! It is perfect for me and

# An Unfinished Story

for you!" Joanie said, gesturing to Carly. "And you need to stay," she turned to John, "because it involved you too!"

Carly leaned against the kitchen counter, sipping her steaming mug of coffee. "What is it?"

"Okay. Listen. You go with him and I stay here with Joe and take care of this place!" Joanie spilled the news like an overflowing bucket.

"But I can't do that. I have to stay here. It's in the will," Carly said sadly.

"No, it's not!" Joanie exclaimed. "The will says you can't sell, but it doesn't say anything about you staying on this island. It says it has to stay in the family. Joe is your family! If you feel guilty about leaving the inn to a complete stranger----me----don't! Joe agreed to help me anytime I need help!"

John rubbed Carly's back and Carly stood up straight.

"But..." she began, "You don't know anything about running a bed and breakfast."

"Oh please!" Joanie replied. "How hard can it really be? Plus, we have a few more weeks until Labor Day, which is when things considerably slow down. You can teach me for the last of the summer season, and then head off to Maine or wherever you want to go in the fall, and I will slowly work my way into running this place during the slow season!" Carly stared at her blankly, processing the idea. "Plus," Joanie continued, "we are just a phone call away! If I truly run into a problem, I will call you! Don't you see? This is your ticket to living the life you want and the life you deserve! You guys deserve to be together. Your story never ended, you guys, it was just paused because life happened. It never ended!"

Carly started crying quietly into her hands, leaning on the granite countertop. Joe rubbed her back and pulled her into a hug. "Carly," Joe whispered, "I have to go."

Carly nodded, told Joanie she needed some time to think, and they exited the house to say one last good-bye. Joanie watched them walk down the deserted, narrow road toward town until they disappeared into the horizon. She felt defeated, but at least she poured her idea out like it was her final lifeline. If this didn't work, she didn't know what she was going to do. Joanie walked back to the carriage house to find Joe drinking a cup of coffee at the kitchen table. Joanie joined him and recounted her conversation with John and Carly. They decided the best thing they could do was enjoy their time, because neither of them knew how much longer they had together.

# Epilogue...6 months later

\*\*\*\*\*\*\*\*\*\*\*\*\*\*\*\*\*\*\*\*\*\*\*\*\*\*\*\*\*\*\*\*\*\*\*\*\*\*\*\*\*\*\*\*\*\*\*\*\*\*\*\*\*\*\*\*\*\*\*\*\*\*\*\*\*\*\*\*\*\*\*\*\*\*\*\*\*\*\*\*\*\*\*\*\*\*\*\*\*\*\*\*\*\*\*\*\*\*

"Welcome to breakfast at The Willowside Inn!" Joanie bellowed as she entered the nearly empty dining room. Her sister, Maria, gave her a smile. Maria held up her coffee mug and clinked mugs with Chris.

"Cheers!" she said.

Joanie walked over to their table with two plates full of pancakes, bacon, sausage, home fries and scrambled eggs. She placed the plates in front of her family and pulled a chair over, waiting for a reaction to the first bite.

"Yum!" Maria exclaimed. "I had no idea you could cook!"

"I couldn't, and I was terrible at it when I first started, but Carly was patient with me and taught me well! You have no idea how many breakfast dinners Joe and I have had so I could perfect my technique. This is pretty much all I can cook without burning down the kitchen. Chris, what do you think?" Joanie asked, indirectly asking for compliments.

"So good!" Chris replied. "Ever since I was a kid, I wondered what it was like to stay here. Carly and I were in different classes, so we didn't really hang out, but every time my parents had friends or family over, she always recommended this place."

"I am so happy you guys came! I know the weather is kind of iffy so I totally appreciate you taking the effort to visit." Joanie looked out the window and took in the collision of gray, depressing skies, and glowing bright snow. The road in front

# An Unfinished Story

of the inn was covered in a dusting of snow that had not yet been disturbed by tire tracks. It was beautiful.

"Of course," Maria answered. "How was Mom and Dad's visit?" Joanie's parents made a trip to New England for Christmas and came to the island for two nights.

"They were shocked that my life had turned in the direction it had. I was so nervous to have them here because they have never been proud or excited for my life choices, but I think they had a good time. There were no kinks and I made Carly and John come back for that weekend, just in case I totally screwed something up and Mom and Dad had more reason to believe that my life was going down the toilet."

Maria smiled. "I stopped caring a long time ago about what they thought of me. They weren't excited when Chris and I moved in together because we weren't married. They weren't excited when I bought an over the top expensive car even though I was working at Kohl's. They weren't excited when I moved halfway across the country to get away from them. It's okay, Joanie. We all make our choices, and as long as you are okay with them, then who cares what they think?"

Joanie always admired how confident her sister was, even when the confidence was fake. "Yeah, I guess we are all just faking life, right? Trying to get through the days the best we can. You're right though. I am happy. I am happy that I got myself out of Boston, happy I got myself out of the media, and happy that I pushed myself out of my comfort zone. I really do love it here. Even though it's been slow because of the weather and the time of year, I feel like I am making a difference, even if that difference is just making people's visits and vacations a little more enjoyable."

"So tell me about Joe," Chris said. "I had no idea you were dating him until Maria showed me a picture of you two at Thanksgiving. He was older than me so I didn't really know him, but I do remember seeing him at Carly's when we were kids. He seemed like a good guy."

"Yes! He is such a good guy. He is patient with me, he lets me be me, he makes me laugh, and he has been so helpful with this transition. We are serious but we don't talk about it. I feel like labels complicate things. He still lives at his house and I live here, but he comes over at least three times a week. Sometimes he comes over as my manager," Joanie airquoted that word, "or he comes over as my boyfriend," Joanie airquoted that word too.

"Do you think he could be the one?" Maria asked

"Honestly, I don't know. I am going to be forty in a few months. I have kind of given up on marriage but if he and I can enjoy each other's company then I am happy. I don't need a husband, I just need a partner. So far, he has come through for me in every crisis. He's amazing."

"Where is he now?" Chris asked.

"He worked the overnight shift. I think he will be coming over after he naps and showers. Usually he comes in around 1 or so. You'll see him before you leave tomorrow. Don't worry!" Joanie said.

That morning, the three of them watched the snow fall, had hot chocolate, and watched movies. Joe came over at 2, just as Joanie had predicted. They kissed each other when he walked in and Joe gave Chris a bro hug. They cooked dinner together and the four of them spent the night playing cards.

Joanie felt amazing and couldn't believe how her life had changed in less than a year. Even if her and Joe didn't work out, she knew that their time together was for the best. She no longer felt stuck in a life that felt out of her control. She no longer felt paralyzed in a job she hated. She no longer felt isolated with no one to talk to. Even if this job didn't work out, she knew that her willingness to change helped Carly chase her dreams. Joanie smiled to herself and poured herself another glass of orange juice.

****************************************************************************************************

"John! Can you grab me a beer?" Carly yelled into the kitchen. She was curled up on the couch, under a blanket, binging the latest drama. They had been inside for twenty-four hours because a Nor'easter had hit and dumped twelve inches of snow. Carly missed these days where she could sit and do nothing. She didn't have to do laundry for other people, cook other people's food, or spend half the day traveling to see her mother. Sometimes stopping was the best thing she could do to take care of herself.

Moving in with John was one of the scariest things she had done. As much as she wanted to leave the island, the idea of actually leaving terrified her. She wasn't happy running the inn, but it was comfortable and predictable, and she was good at it. Leaving meant starting over in a new city with no job with a man she hadn't intertwined her life with in nine years. Carly at age 30 was very different from Carly at age 39. A lot of life had happened for both of them, and there was no guarantee that they would mesh the way they remembered.

Carly's mother had left her some money, which gave her the courage to pack up and leave. Even if it was the worst decision and her entire life crumbled in this foreign place, she could still return home. She still had a home that was fully paid for. She could still go back to the life she had been living.

Carly hung around the inn until October, which was enough time for her to feel confident that Joanie and Joe could manage. John came back to Maine and worked until Lobster season was over without Carly. They decided that it was best if they found an apartment together instead of Carly moving into John's place. It would allow them both to leave their past behind and create a new life together. Plus, John was a bachelor, so he was living in a studio the size of Carly's bedroom at home.

They found a cute two bedroom apartment overlooking the harbor within walking distance to all the shops and restaurants. Carly didn't want to overpower the planning, so they compromised and filled their apartment with just the basics. Carly found a job waitressing at her old restaurant, which helped her transition back into her old life. The old friends she had had all moved on, but at least she was familiar with the menu.

John's work completely ended when Carly moved back, so they were able to spend time reconnecting and getting to know each other again. He picked up a side job driving for Uber and worked when Carly worked, so they were able to see each other as often as possible.

John sat down next to Carly and gave her a local craft beer bottle. They watched seven hours of TV together, curled up under the blanket on the couch. Carly knew that life wouldn't be like this forever, but did her best to be brave and enjoy every single moment. Life could change as quickly as the weather, and Carly knew that every weather phenomenon had beauty if you looked hard enough. At that moment, she felt joy in recognizing the beauty of her situation.

# Meet Erica Haraldsen

Erica Haraldsen lives with her husband, two children, and three furbabies in Massachusetts. She always enjoyed writing short stories and writing in a journal when she was a child. She majored in Journalism for a hot second in college and graduated with a masters in Speech-language pathology. For most of her adult years, her writing was placed on the back burner due to the chaos of full time parenting and full time work. With a little encouragement, she decided to write a novel, write it well, and write it scared. This is her debut novel and through her writing, she hopes to convey themes that are relatable to all women. She hopes her books are enjoyed by all who read them. She thanks you for reading and is truly honored.

Made in the USA
Middletown, DE
02 May 2020